Young Hoosier Book Award

Association for Indiana Media Educators

06-07

CHIG

AND THE SECOND SPREAD

GWENYTH SWAIN

CHIG

AND THE SECOND SPREAD

Delacorte Press

Published by
Delacorte Press
an imprint of
Random House Children's Books
a division of Random House, Inc.
New York

Visit us on the Web! www.randomhouse.com/kids
Educators and librarians, for a variety of teaching tools, visit us at
www.randomhouse.com/teachers

Library of Congress Cataloging-in-Publication Data
Swain, Gwenyth.
Chig & the second spread / Gwenyth Swain.
p. cm.
Summary: Despite her small stature, eight-year-old Chig makes large
contributions to her southern Indiana community during the Great Depression.
ISBN 0-385-73065-9 (trade)—ISBN 0-385-90094-5 (GLB)
[1. Growth—Fiction.   2. Size—Fiction.   3. Railroad accidents—Fiction.
4. Poor—Fiction.   5. Depressions—1929—Fiction.   6. Indiana—History—
20th century—Fiction.   7. Roosevelt, Eleanor, 1884–1962—Fiction.]
I. Title: Chig and the second spread.   II. Title.
PZ7.S969893Ch 2003
[Fic]—dc21   2003003631

The text of this book is set in 12-point Joanna MT.

Book design by Angela Carlino

Printed in the United States of America

November 2003

10 9 8 7 6 5 4 3 2 1

BVG

For my father, Henry Swain, whose stories
of growing up during the Great Depression
I have so shamelessly stolen

For the late Genevra Irene ("Chig") Owens,
first female county commissioner of
Brown County, Indiana, whose nickname
I have respectfully borrowed

ACKNOWLEDGMENTS

I am grateful to the following people for their help in making this story better: Jill Anderson, Angela Carlino, Earl Vincent Dolan III, Colleen Fellingham, Tom Fletcher, Wendy Loggia, Karen Mereck, Kevin Morrissey, Pat Schmatz and the rest of the Monday Night Group, Margaret Coman Swain, Roger Tea, and Jane Resh Thomas. And although they didn't do it on my account, I'd like to thank my parents for not making it all the way out west and settling instead on forty acres in the hills of Brown County.

CONTENTS

1

CHIGGER

Way down deep in the hills and hollers of southern Indiana, there once was a girl named Chig. No, Chig was not her real name. But when her daddy first laid eyes on her, he said, "That girl ain't any bigger than a little red chigger."

She was small, but well proportioned. Plain, but in a pleasing way. A sturdy baby, with a crown of frizzy red hair and eyes as soft and green as the leaves on a dogtooth violet. "It's the eyes," her mama said. "They're what make her almost, near-about pretty."

As the years passed and she grew older, her daddy allowed as how she'd grown. "'Bout the size of a chigger bite that's been scratched a few times too many," he said, looking her up and down. But as big as she got—and that wasn't any too large—she never outgrew her nickname.

"Chigger" seemed almost too big for her, so folks took to calling her Chig. And before anyone had any time to give it any thought, they'd all forgotten that her real name was Minerva.

This couldn't have mattered less to Chig. "We all got to have a name," she told her teacher, Miss Barkus, when she started school. "Might as well have one that fits."

Miss Barkus, Chig noticed, wasn't like most grown-ups. She was broad as a barrel and taller than a sumac tree run wild. But she didn't peer down distractedly at Chig like people generally did. Miss Barkus eased herself lower, knees creaking under the pressure of her bulk. When she was eye level with Chig, and considerably lower than anyone else's ears, she said, "You know what, Minerva? That's a grand nickname you've got. Wish I'd had one just as good when I was your age." Then she adjusted her voice so that the whole room could hear. "We'll register you as Chig M. Kalpin."

Chig beamed. Then she started. There was a commotion of slapping and snickering somewhere behind her. When she turned toward the back of the room, she saw several near-grown boys swatting each other and scratching their armpits and kneepits as if they were being worried by a swarm of chiggers. Chig's own daddy had given her play chigger-bite pinches when she was a baby girl, and she grinned at the memory. But the boys didn't grin back in a friendly way.

"Silence!" With that simple, sharp command from Miss Barkus, all snickering and swatting stopped. Chig felt her teacher's warmest smile shining on her, and she dared to continue their talk. "But why would you want a nickname?" she asked. "Miss Barkus suits you fine." Her voice was so soft and small, it was possible no one heard her, Miss Barkus included. That had happened more times than Chig could count. But her teacher surprised her. Still hunched on creaking knees, she whispered, "It's my first name that doesn't suit."

Chig blinked. Somehow Miss Barkus read the question in her eyes.

"It's Lily," she went on. "Can you imagine putting a name that delicate on someone like me?"

But before Chig could muster up an answer, her teacher swept on to another question. "Your birth date?" Miss Barkus asked.

Chig swallowed hard. Her answer was likely to get her in trouble. "It's the first of April," she said, "nineteen twenty-five."

It wasn't being an April fool that was so troublesome. It was her age.

"But that'd make you eight, Chig," said Miss Barkus. "What's taken you so long getting here? School's not so far from home you couldn't have come last year or the year before, is it?"

How could she explain? How her parents had held her back the first year, hoping she might grow a wee bit taller or bigger. How Mama's eyes had welled up, near to bursting with tears, the previous fall. "It's not easy being the oldest," Mama warned, "with no one to show you the ropes at school. Plus, kids can be hard on you when you're different." Chig guessed *different* meant small.

"Couldn't we hold her back one more year," Mama pleaded with Daddy, "just in case she gets a spurt?"

Daddy agreed, and for another year Chig helped Mama with chores and kept her younger brother, Hubert, from jumping off the henhouse roof. To make sure Chig wouldn't be too far behind once her growth spurt came, Mama taught her the letters of the alphabet, all the numbers from one to twenty-six ("So you'll know as much math as you do letters," Mama explained), and how to write her name.

Maybe in some other, more traveled corner of the world, a government official would have investigated and ordered Chig to school, small as she was. But Chig's corner, around the town of Niplak, was decidedly less traveled. No one there had seen a government official in years, and the natives tended to mind their own business.

Mama and Daddy watched Chig closely, but they saw no sign of a spurt. "'Fraid you'll have to face the world as you are," Daddy had decided at last.

"Well," said Miss Barkus, taking Chig's silence as a kind of answer, "I've never been one to push folks into doing what they're not ready for. There's a big river of learning out there, and we're not all willing to get our feet wet at the same time. You feeling ready now, Chig?"

Chig glanced at her feet, dry and warm, if a little un-comfortable in shoes after a long summer spent running bare-soled. Was her teacher talking about a real river or creek? Full of mud and crawdads? Probably not. "I could get my feet wet," she said.

Miss Barkus's smile showed Chig that this answer, at least, was the right one. "You're not afraid of hard work, are you?"

"Nope."

"You'll have a lot of catching up to do, to have lessons with the other eight-year-olds."

"I don't mind catch-up," said Chig. She liked ketchup, too, but didn't think this was the time to mention it.

"And starting tomorrow," Miss Barkus said, "you'll have to sit out recesses this fall and winter while we get you up to steam."

"But there'll be more recesses in the spring?" Chig

asked. She'd heard about recess from friends at Sunday school and didn't want to miss out on it altogether.

"You bet," said Miss Barkus. Then she steered Chig to the smallest desk in the classroom.

Chig studied its wrought-iron base—much like the one on her mama's sewing machine—and its hinged wooden top. Generations of county boys and girls had sat at that very desk. Most had tried to make their mark on it with a pocketknife. None had left a name as good as Chig. Her fingers itched to try.

Chig's gaze roamed every square inch of the room. Behind her, the students in each row got bigger and older. Some Chig knew from the Church of Our Redeemer, like Alberta Beemis. Others, like Jimbo and Theo Limp, she'd seen in town on Saturday nights, when folks went to do their shopping and talking for the week. A few were total strangers from hollers so far off the beaten path they probably weren't on any map.

To Chig's right was a scrawny, sleepy-eyed boy. Surely a Huddleston, from the looks of him. "Willy Huddleston," he said when Chig whispered "Hey" to him. Seated beyond him was a girl perhaps Chig's age whose head drooped under the weight of her hair. Her chestnut braids scraped the floor. "It's never been cut," Alberta Beemis whispered to Chig later. "Their church don't allow cutting, for Biblical reasons."

The wonders of the one-room schoolhouse didn't stop there. In all, Miss Barkus registered twenty-one scholars, as she liked to call them. They came in all shapes and sizes, but none was so small as Chig. The youngest of the younguns sitting in Chig's row were a good head taller than she was. It was a situation she'd been in before.

At the Church of Our Redeemer, a visiting preacher had tried once to herd Chig into the baby class with Hubert. "I'm no baby!" she'd said, pulling away from Hubie and the other droolers.

"It's a miracle!" the preacher had yelled. "The Lord has made this baby talk!" (Alberta still called Chig Miracle Baby from time to time, but she said it in a friendly way.) Alberta and the Limp twins and Willy Huddleston looked as if they might soon be as huge as some of the near-grown scholars who lurked in the back row. But Chig remained petite. That word had been the centerpiece of Chig's mama's morning pep talk.

"It's French," Mama said, as if she were arming Chig with something exotic and special. "And it means you're normal for you. Small compared to others, maybe, but all in the right proportions."

Had Miss Barkus heard about *petite*? Maybe it didn't matter. Chig had the decided feeling that when Miss Barkus led the way to the river of learning, she didn't judge her scholars by size. Chig Kalpin settled in to get her feet good and wet.

Miss Barkus pulled down a color map of Our Nation, on which she had drawn the boundaries of all states added after 1901, when the map had been made in Chicago, Illinois. Chig nodded and followed Miss Barkus's pointer. It tapped its way down the sock shape of Lake Michigan to the top of Indiana. Down, down, down it tapped until the pointer rested on their very own Culpepper County. Still recognizable, although the color had worn a bit thin from so much tapping through the years.

Morning raced by like an express train, and soon, having munched their lunches, the scholars chugged out to the schoolyard at full steam for recess.

"Hey, Chig," Alberta Beemis called, "wanna jump rope?"

"Yep," Chig answered, and she took her place holding the ropes for double Dutch. But she didn't plan to stay long. Alberta, as Chig knew from Sunday school, was a chatterbox. Big talkers like Alberta might be nice and all, but they were the kind of folks who knew no economy. They'd likely fry bacon and throw out the fat. Plus, there was so much to see. Why spend her only recess until who-knew-when talking?

When the girl with the long hair came near, Chig smiled and handed her the rope. Soon she was pumping so hard her braids were hopping. Chig backed away and nearly landed in a game of hopscotch. At school, it seemed, people were thicker than rocks on a creek bottom.

"Isn't that a Kalpin?" Alberta's big brother Ed asked. Of all the boys in the back of Miss Barkus's classroom, Ed Beemis was the flashiest. He was only twelve but tall and solid. He swaggered more than walked. Unlike the other boys, who came to school in patched overalls, Ed wore pants and sported a red bandana in his back pocket. This he pulled out with a flourish every time he sneezed. Rumor had it Ed's mama washed and pressed enough so that he had a new, clean hanky for every day of the week. What luxury!

Chig stopped in her tracks and nodded to Ed and the cluster of boys draped around and over the big sycamore tree. At church, Ed was always too busy singing in the choir or doing the weekly scripture reading to take much notice of Chig.

"Cat got yer tongue?" Ed said. He poked another boy in the ribs when Chig nodded.

"Who you talking to, Ed?" someone asked. "I don't see anything over there but a chigger."

"She is mighty small," Ed agreed. "The runt of the litter, for sure."

"Yep," said one boy, "a runty old chigger."

"And you know what happens to runts . . . ," said Ed, nodding darkly at Chig.

Somehow, the way those laughing and rib-poking boys called her Chigger didn't make Chig feel precious the way it did when Daddy said it. And the way they said runt filled her mind with images of a pig too weak to feed— the kind of pig a farmer less softhearted than Mr. Kalpin would kill in an instant. "For its own good," a sensible farmer would say. "Put it out of its misery." Ed Beemis in particular seemed to have sized Chig up the same as a runt pig. Not worth the money you'd spend on its feed.

Folks had kidded Chig about her size before. Some of her very own cousins called her Shorty Jr., but that made sense since they also called Chig's granny Shorty—and everyone agreed Chig took after Granny Shorty Kalpin. But never before had Chig been called a name and felt a sting of pain.

"I'm petite!" Chig said, finally finding her voice.

But the boys just laughed. "Pah-*teet*!" Ed roared. "She says she's pah-*teet*! Ain't that a fine name for a runty little pig." He said it just the way Chig's daddy said "Su-*keey*!" when he yelled after hogs.

Miss Barkus's silver bell, pealing in the air, called the scholars back into the schoolhouse. But it could not could pull Chig out of her misery. *Snort! Snort! Snort!* she heard behind her.

Ed was awfully convincing. Chig looked around to see whose hog had gotten loose, only to see his smirking face. She hurried inside to the safety of the smallest desk.

Chig slid into her seat like liver onto a cold plate. Not even the feel of worn wood under her fingertips or the smell of chalk on the board could make her lift her eyes. Next to her, Willy Huddleston nodded, but she barely saw him. "Hey," he said as the other scholars found their places.

"Hey," Chig answered. She and Willy had exchanged heys before, but Chig sensed Willy was warming up for a longer conversation.

"Out at our place, we can't afford to lose a hog," he said softly, "not even the runts. Mama and me, we fatten them up on corn mash and goat's milk. You'd be surprised the sweet hams you can get out of a runt if you treat it right."

"I expect that's true," Chig said.

A little warm goat's milk would be just the thing to calm her stomach. It felt pinched and achy. But soon Miss Barkus distracted her and the other scholars, urging them all to stick a toe in the river of learning.

2

SHRINKAGE

Hubie couldn't get enough of school. Each day when Chig came home, he asked her to tell him every detail. She tried to oblige, telling him, for example, how scholars earned stars. "The silver ones mean 'very fine, but you can improve,'" she explained, holding her latest paper. Miss Barkus had marked it, as usual, with a shimmery lick-on star. It was hardly even much worse for wear for having been clutched in Chig's hand during the half-mile walk over dirt roads and across the brambly path. Mama found two pushpins and stuck the paper to the mantelpiece, high enough so that Hubie, who was four and a half and a climber, couldn't get at it.

"Bring me home more stars," Hubie begged, and Chig did her best. She too liked the way they shimmered in the glow of the kerosene lamp on the mantel. The Kalpin home was bare of much decoration. Chig's sheets of brown lined paper, torn carefully from the thick pad in Teacher's top side desk drawer and decorated with stars, lent the front room a festive air.

"If I loan you my pocketknife, will you carve my name in your desk so's it'll be ready for me when I go?" he asked.

"Too busy, Hubie," she answered. "Got no time for carving when there's so much catch-up to do."

Hubie let it go at that, but he asked again and again for Chig to tell him about recess. Even the four-year-old Sunday school class had heard about that. Ever since the second day of school, Chig had been spending recess inside, playing catch-up with Miss Barkus. She'd only played with the other scholars once. Sometimes, when Hubie asked, Chig thought she should tell him the whole story so he'd know what to expect. But the picture she painted for her brother was sunny and warm, just like the afternoon on that first day of school.

Why tell him that whenever she walked by the back-row boys, they started scratching at imaginary chigger bites? Why let him know that she'd heard more snorts than could be explained by loose hogs wandering in the woods by the schoolyard? Why say that, in her humble opinion, Ed Beemis was a lot better Christian on church property than off?

Mama must have sensed that Chig was holding something back. Or maybe having another youngun on the way made Mama nostalgic for the old days when she'd been young herself. That fall, Mrs. Kalpin spent evenings after supper in the family's easy chair by the fire, her feet propped up, her belly so big Chig thought it might explode. The baby was due just before Christmas.

"Did I ever tell you how I met your daddy?" Mrs. Kalpin asked one evening after Hubie had gone to bed and while Daddy was out working on the tractor.

Chig knew the story from Daddy but didn't say so. Mama hardly ever chatted. Like Chig, she'd been born short on words. Chig perched on the edge of Mama's footstool.

Mama went on. "Your granddaddy Lukens was asked to come down from Indianapolis to preach at a revival in Bear Hollow, just over the hill from Niplak," Mama said, "and I went along. Your daddy caught my eye when I was singing in the choir. Then he grabbed the seat right next to me at the church supper."

Mama paused to catch her breath after such a long speech. She coaxed a few snarls out of Chig's frizzy red hair.

"Know what was so special about Daddy?" Mama asked.

Chig sat up straighter. This was a part of the story she hadn't heard before.

"It was how he treated me," Mama said. "We Lukens are good country folk. Course our ancestors used to live in Niplak before Granddaddy Lukens got the call to minister to heathens in the city."

Chig felt a sharp tug at her hair.

"Sorry, dearie," Mama said. Then she settled back into her story. "You can't know how it was for me to go to school up in Indianapolis. I was the oldest, so no one at home could tell me what to expect. I didn't know they'd call me Hillbilly soon as I opened my mouth to speak."

Mama sighed, and Chig leaned softly into her warm, round belly.

"Your daddy never called me anything but Miss Lukens until we were married and I managed to get him to say Meg. And he's never treated anybody any way but decent."

"Daddy's good people," Chig agreed.

"Way down deep," Mama said, "I think—whatever folks may call us, whatever we call folks—we all got an equal chance to be decent. We're just not all of us as ready as we could be."

Chig considered this for a moment and said the first

thing that popped into her head. "Willy Huddleston told me if you treat a runt pig decent, it'll grow to be a sweet ham."

Mama was so startled she gave Chig a quick goodnight hug, and their talk ended as suddenly as it had begun.

Playing catch-up with Miss Barkus wasn't easy, but Chig made steady progress.

"Fine work, Chig," Miss Barkus said. "You're on track to join the other eight-year-olds and have a real recess come spring."

Chig smiled at the thought of taking lessons with Alberta and the other scholars her age. But recess . . . Would a spurt come along by spring so she wouldn't feel quite so small, measured up against the Ed Beemises of the world?

At home one night that fall, Chig stayed on with Daddy in the barn after her chores were done. She watched him clean a paintbrush he'd been using. The stiff, sharp scent of turpentine filled the air.

"How's business, Chig?" Daddy asked.

"Could be better," she answered. One by one, she picked up the tin cans lining Daddy's workbench and studied their contents. Nails, screws, rubber gaskets, even blue jay feathers. She would have given them all her closest attention, but Daddy didn't let her.

"Care to fill me in?" he asked.

Chig sighed. What good would talking do? It might only use up energy she could put into growing. Then again, Daddy usually had the answers.

"Why am I so small?" she asked. A picture flashed in her mind of her own self at school, the smallest of all the scholars, the runt of the litter.

"Ah," Daddy said, "my little chigger's impatient to grow, is she?"

Chig nodded.

"Well," Daddy began, "there's folks born to bigness, and others born to smallness. And then, of course, there's a whole mess of folks in between."

Chig leaned forward on her stool and set the tin cans aside.

"Now, Granny Shorty Kalpin, my mama, she's one born to smallness. Why, she never weighed more than ninety-nine pounds until she birthed me and your uncle Elwin—and we were ten-pound twins."

"Are you sure I take after Granny?" Chig asked.

"It's early days yet," Daddy said, "but I'm guessing you might take more after her than someone born to bigness, like me or your mama. But like I say, it's early days yet."

"So I might catch up?" Chig asked.

"Stranger things have happened," he said. "The way your granny Kalpin tells it, Elwin and me were scrawny boys until we both got a growth spurt. Says she put us to bed one size and when we got up the next morning, we'd both outgrown our trousers."

"That so?" Chig asked. Granny was a dear-heart, but she'd been known to put stretchers into her stories.

"That's how Granny tells it," Daddy said.

Chig awoke the next morning feeling hopeful, but no spurt had hit her in the night. Nearly every month Hubie asked to be measured—and nearly every month he was bigger. Chig knew from experience that monthly measurements were bound to bring disappointment in her case. She had long before settled for annual measurings, and usually the results were good, or as good as could be expected. But according to records kept carefully on the inside of a closet door at the home place, Chig appeared to be shrinking.

She grabbed a ruler and double-checked. But the pencil markings Mama had made on the closet door didn't lie. Between her seventh and eighth falls, Chig had lost about an eighth of an inch. Her heels had been planted firmly on the ground, her head facing forward. "Don't look up," Mama always warned. But Chig was too honest about her smallness to need the warning.

For a day or so, Chig puzzled over her shrinkage. Then she remembered. Her last measuring had taken place on a Saturday evening, just after her weekly bath. The year before, she'd been measured in the morning, when she was dry.

Chig's hair, when dry, was frizzy enough to push a pencil up at least half an inch. To set the record straight, she sharpened a good point and made the following additions:

Chig M. Kalpin, age 7, Nov. 1, 1932 ———— (DRY)

Chig M. Kalpin, age 8, Nov. 8, 1933 ———— (WET)

3

SHORT WAYS TO SAY SOMETHING BIG

Chig had her work cut out for her if she was going to catch up when it came to size. But the more she got her feet wet in the river of learning, the more she began to think that, maybe, she could help herself along.

Her first efforts were not particularly successful. One day, she covered the gray of her slate with all the biggest words she'd learned at school so far: *vowel, privy, tobacco*. Then she wrote the most impressive names she knew: FDR, FERA. That was when she had the brainstorm. What made FDR and FERA seem so big and powerful? Why, the fact that they were all capital letters.

CHIG. She let the swirls and loops of the capital letters

spool out in chalk. Much more impressive than plain old Chig. For a whole day, she signed her schoolwork that way, and for a whole day it made her feel bigger, almost. Miss Barkus brought her back down to earth.

"Chig," she asked at recess the next day, "may I ask why you've changed the way you sign your name?"

"It's taller that way."

"Sure it is," said Miss Barkus, "but we don't usually spell our names in all capitals, do we?"

"Some folks do," Chig answered. "There's FDR and FERA. Think how small they'd feel if they weren't all tall letters."

"But they're not tall so much as they're short for something," said Miss Barkus. "See." Chig's teacher wrote the letters across the chalkboard. Then she filled in what they stood for.

FDR was, Chig discovered, just a tallish short way of saying Franklin Delano Roosevelt.

Turned out, either way you wrote it, he was still the nation's president. FERA was nothing more than a quick way of saying a mouthful.

"It stands for Federal Emergency Relief Administration," Miss Barkus said, "a new government agency in Washington."

Chig nodded. Now that she heard her teacher say them, the names and words behind the tall letters sure sounded familiar. Come to think of it, hadn't she heard them on the radio more than once?

"So you see, the letters all stand for something," Miss Barkus said.

"But . . . ," Chig began.

"But what?"

"But what if a person got to be as famous as FDR? Then could they go by all tall letters?" Chig asked.

Miss Barkus paused, her eraser stopped midswipe. "If you become as famous as our president, then I would be honored to call you CMK, for Chig M. Kalpin."

With that, she quickly drew the letters, so big they almost filled the board. Chig admired her teacher's handiwork. It nearly took her breath away.

"Well," said Chig at last, "I'll work on making the letters stand for something."

"Excellent idea," said Miss Barkus, sweeping the board clean. "In the meantime, I suggest you study the news and news makers of the day. It can be quite an alphabet soup at first, but I'm sure you'll make sense of it."

Chig nodded. She'd been reading and writing like a house afire since the first few weeks of school. Her feet were certainly wet with learning, but she could see she needed to wade a bit deeper into the creek.

The radio crackled as the batteries inside warmed up and the signal from Chicago came in. Hubie inched closer to Chig on the kitchen bench. Her brother liked to act the part of a big, brave almost-five-year-old, and he surely was big, nearly Chig's height. But radio sound effects, and even bursts of static, scared the daylights out of him. So as soon as the dial clicked on for the evening news, Hubie sat as near as he could without landing in Chig's lap. Lately, she'd been listening closely to the news. But tonight the Reverend Granddaddy Lukens was firmly at the controls.

"You don't mind a little company, do you?" he'd asked when he knocked at the door. Granddaddy Lukens was an ordained minister of the Evangelical Crucifixion and Resurrection faith, and church business had sent him to a meeting of reverends in Seymour. "I decided to take the scenic route home. Didn't want to miss the chance to see my favorite oldest daughter and the best grandkids this side of the Mississippi."

He hugged Chig hard and set her on a tabletop. "That's more like it," he said. "We always see eye to eye, don't we, girlie?"

Mama insisted on cooking something extra nice for her daddy, who so rarely visited. Granddaddy Lukens tried to dissuade her, large and slow with pregnancy as she was, but he finally gave up. He settled into the easy chair, Hubie perched on one arm, Chig on the other. "Your mother's always been a stubborn cuss," he said. "Can't think where she gets it."

"Oh, can't you?" Mama asked from the kitchen.

Knowing a meal of good country cooking awaited him, Chig's granddaddy was in extra-high spirits. With his frizzy white whiskers and cherry red cheeks, Chig thought he looked more like a Santy Claus than a preacher. And sometimes, Chig decided, he didn't even *sound* like a preacher.

When Lowell Thomas started reading the news, Granddaddy grabbed the dial and switched over to the Pittsburgh station without so much as a pardon me.

"If I hear one more dadblasted reporter talking about the president and how he's pulling us out of this depression, I think I'll burst a gasket!" he roared. "I'd rather listen to an ad for Tasty Yeast any day."

Chig loved the Tasty Yeast song and often caught herself humming its catchy tune. But not now. Granddaddy looked to be a good source of information on news and alphabet soup, so Chig set to questioning him.

"You seen much of the depression?" Chig asked. She'd heard a lot about the depression since she'd been paying attention to the news, but it seemed far away. Granddaddy lived fifty miles north in a big city. Maybe things were different there.

"Surely I have," he answered. "You only have to look

on the street corners to find grown men selling apples for a living."

"Apples?" Chig asked. "But don't they have trees in their yards?"

"Not in the city, dearie," he said. "And for many, that's the best job they can find. You could even call them lucky. At least they aren't throwing themselves out of windows or living the life of a hobo riding the rails."

"Throwing themselves out of windows?" Hubie asked. When he wasn't climbing, Hubie was usually jumping. Mama didn't like to encourage either, Chig knew. She wasn't surprised when Granddaddy got the Look. Mama's Look meant "No more of that, if you please!" But Chig knew what Granddaddy was talking about. It wasn't anything like jumping off a henhouse roof; there was no joy in it. She'd read in the newspaper kept in the schoolhouse library corner about businessmen in Chicago who leaped out the windows of skyscrapers to their deaths.

"Why would anybody do such a thing?" she'd asked Miss Barkus one recess.

"Sometimes the future is more than a person can face" was all Miss Barkus would say.

The paper said the men hadn't worked much but had made lots of money anyhow. Then, all of a sudden, they'd lost every penny. Chig had never had much money. For as long as anyone could remember, hardly a soul in

Culpepper County had ever had cash to speak of. Maybe that made people around Niplak lucky. What they'd never had, they couldn't miss. And with everyone in the same boat and not feeling lonesome, the future couldn't look too bad.

Most men around Niplak had half a dozen jobs, not just one. Chig's daddy could usually count on a few months' work with the county road crew in good weather. Then there were the family's acres of bottom-land to farm in his spare time, spring, summer, and fall. Other times he filled in with odd jobs painting houses and harvesting Christmas trees. Granddaddy Lukens's depression in Indianapolis didn't sound half as lucky as Chig's was.

"If you saw the looks on the men's faces," he was saying to Mama, "you'd want to take the folks in Washington by the shoulders and say, 'Will we ever get out of this?'" He stopped and rubbed his whiskery chin.

"See many hoboes?" Chig asked. She'd heard about them too but had never caught sight of one in Niplak.

"More than you can count, Chig," Granddaddy said. "They stop at my back porch before hopping a freight car out of town." He shook his head sadly. "When you're a preacher, they'll find you. I've seen their markings on my gate."

"Markings?" Chig asked. "What're they?"

"They're messages for the other hoboes," Grandaddy said. "And they mean 'Here's a good place for a meal!'"

He sniffed at Mama's good cooking. "Surprised you don't have markings on your own gate. Course, I don't mind feeding the men what I have. I look at them sometimes and think I see the face of Christ, all hungry and tired and ignored on the cross."

"Daddy," Mama called from the stove. "Maybe that's enough truth-telling for one night."

"Oh, Mama," Chig pleaded, "please don't make the Reverend Granddaddy stop!"

"The Reverend Granddaddy!" Mama cried. "You're not making the children call you that, are you, Daddy?"

"It's a hard world, Meg Kalpin," Granddaddy said, winking at Chig. "We got to find our happiness where we may."

He pushed Chig gently off the chair. "Now, go on, scoot! Help your mama fix one of her world-famous suppers."

Something about that fine supper, or the hard work that went into it, hurried the new baby along. Granddaddy Lukens had only been gone a few hours Saturday morning when Mama sat down hard in her kitchen rocker. Daddy was cutting Christmas trees. He'd taken Hubie along for company.

"Chig!" Mama said. It was a small cry, full of more worry and fear than Chig liked to hear. She came running at once.

"Oooh," Mama said, her face showing the pain all too clearly. "This baby wants to come soon!"

For a moment, Mama almost seemed to stop breathing. She was looking, or not looking, at a point somewhere above Chig's left ear. Chig scratched her ear and waited. Finally, Mama let out a long breath and came back to herself.

"Call Doc Settle," she said, "and ask him to drive out here quick."

Chig lugged a chair over to the wall where the telephone hung. Perched on the seat, she could just pull the receiver off its hook and turn the hand crank to get the batteries going. When the hook popped up and she cupped the receiver to her ear, she could hear Floyd Wild on the party line.

"It's Floyd," Chig told Mama, putting a hand over the mouthpiece. Old Floyd loved to be the bearer of news, even news that wasn't his own. When he wasn't listening in on other people's conversations, he was broadcasting his voice over the phone lines.

"Tell him I'm having a baby and he can't tie up the line," Mama said.

Chig turned back and tried her best. "Oh, Mr. Wild," she said. "This is Chig Kalpin, and my mama is having a baby."

"Anyone with two eyes in their head can see that," Floyd said. "Now, either tell me something I don't know or kindly get off the line." With that, Floyd picked up his chatting where he'd left off.

Chig tried again. "Bet you don't know my mama's having her baby *right now*, in the kitchen rocker."

That stopped Floyd's flow of words. "Where's your daddy, Chig? Does he know about this?"

"He's out at Miller's tree farm with Hubie, Mr. Wild," Chig answered, "and we'd be obliged if you'd get a message up to them to come straight home."

"Will do." Click.

Chig's call to Doc Settle went smoothly, but while she waited for him to arrive, things got rough.

"Clear the daybed, Chig!" Mama cried, her voice rising.

"Throw that old quilt on top!"

"Help me over there, girlie!"

"Hold my hand! *Please?*"

The last request was so unexpected Chig wasn't sure what to do at first. Since when did grown-ups need a hand to hold? And since when did her very own mama sound small and helpless? Chig looked down on her mother, spread out on the low daybed, knees bent, eyes wild.

All Chig could remember of Hubie's birth was being packed off to spend a winter afternoon in her aunt Ida's stuffy kitchen. She'd only ever witnessed the births of calves and kittens and chicks. Hens always looked so satisfied and clucked so contentedly when their babies pecked their way into the world. Mama looked more like Ginger, the barn cat, or Bossie, the cow—scared, sweaty, and anxious. Chig hardly dared touch her for fear of catching some of that scaredness. But finally, tenderly, she reached for Mama's hand and held on tight.

Every few minutes, Mama clamped down on Chig's small hand as if she'd seen something dreadful hovering over the daybed. Chig looked up too, but saw nothing, apart from the usual cracks in the plaster. Always before when she'd read about eternity in the Bible, Chig hadn't known what it meant. Now, gazing up at the ceiling, she felt trapped with Mama in a place of endless time. At last the sound of gravel flying in the drive set time back on its usual course. Doc Settle arrived in such haste that his car nearly skidded into the Kalpin front room with him. He bustled through the doorway and started clucking over Mama.

"You almost beat me to the punch this time, Meg," he said. Then to Chig he added, "Go on into the kitchen for a spell. Start some water on the boil and gather up some clean towels. I'll give a yell when we need you."

"All righty," said Chig, relieved to be relieved. But things didn't seem all right. From what she remembered of Bossie's and Ginger's birthings, things were bound to get messy.

Mama yelled and yelled again, but Chig stayed by the kitchen stove, her feet as heavy as a statue's. Part of her wanted to race to the daybed and help. The other preferred to watch the water boil. With water, you generally knew what to expect.

Finally, Doc Settle cried, "It's a girl!"

And Mama, sounding big and whole and brave again like her old self, said, "It sure is."

Chig grabbed the teakettle and towels so Doc Settle could quickly wash and wrap the new-minted baby. She was messy, all right, but just as sweet and squirmy as a new calf or kitten. While Doc Settle fussed over Mama, Chig held the baby and got a closer look. Her eyes opened uncertainly on the day. Her hair, still matted and wet with birth, looked frizzy and red, just like Chig's. It was too soon to tell if she'd be petite or not, but she was all in the right proportions.

"Hope she'll grow up to be as big a helper as her sister is," Mama said when Daddy and Hubie finally swept into the cabin.

"That'd be a tall order." Daddy winked at Chig before he and Hubie inspected the baby.

Chig was sure she could and should have done more to help, but she smiled all the same at such kind words. "What's her name going to be?" she asked.

"We've talked about Emma," said Mama.

"But we'll call her Em, for short," Daddy said.

"Em," Chig repeated, looking into her sister's eyes. The name was small but oh so fine. A short way to say that in the Kalpin home, each heart was larger than it had been before.

4

LOSING MARBLES

Chig stayed home from school a whole two weeks helping Mama regain her strength and spoiling baby Em. Then it was back to schoolwork in earnest.

Christmas and the New Year distracted the big boys in the back row from their usual taunting. Chig felt almost peaceful inside when she passed Ed and the others on her way to the outhouse that perched on the edge of the nearby creek. As she picked her way down the outhouse path, she thought she could smell an early spring—and recess—in the air.

"I'd say you're near about ready for recess," Miss

Barkus told Chig one day. "You're certainly caught up with the other scholars your age now."

Being all caught up and getting recess to boot was just about the best present Chig thought a girl could have, and it wasn't even close to being her birthday yet. To top it all off, 1934 brought with it a once-in-a-hundred-year spring. Not even the oldest of the old settlers could recall a spring so pleasant or so prompt. One of Chig's extra-elderly great-aunts was heard to say at church, "There's sure to be only bad sprouting out of weather so nice."

Nature seemed bent on proving that great-aunt wrong. There was just enough warmth and wetness in the air to make Chig's small heart sing and to cause flowers and wild mushrooms to spring up in abundance. With all that thawing going on, the schoolyard dirt was still soft for Chig's first recess of the year. Too soft for good jump-roping and hopscotching. But Chig wasn't going to waste her recess leaning on the old sycamore and listening to Alberta talk. A pile of empty cardboard boxes and old planks sat by the trash-burning barrel at one end of the yard. They gave Chig inspiration and a boldness she usually lacked.

"Hey, Alberta," Chig called. "Wanna play Going to Niplak?"

"Huh?" Alberta asked.

"See," Chig explained, "we take these boxes and line

them up, just like the buildings in Niplak. Then we drag these planks along in the dirt and carve roads in the mud."

For once, Alberta didn't say a word. Instead, she raced to the pile of boxes to help Chig get started. Chig loved her hometown of Niplak. How could she help it? Her very own great-great-granddaddy Kalpin had wandered up from Kentucky almost a hundred years before, becoming one of Niplak's founders. He'd plunked a cabin down and made his claim before folks had the time and the sense to see it was no use trying to farm the thin clay dirt of Culpepper County.

Great-great-granddaddy Kalpin didn't let a little bit of bad luck discourage him. He hunkered down and found a way to coax a few acres of sorghum and tobacco out of his land. He did well enough to cut a window into one cabin wall. Shortly thereafter, he married. Then he raised a family of twelve in a space no bigger than the average henhouse.

Somehow he managed to set himself apart from the other dirt-poor farmers in the area, although no one could remember anymore just how. When the locals decided to give their cluster of cabins and lean-tos a name, they hoped to honor Chig's great-great-granddaddy and name the place Kalpinville. But being by nature quiet, shy, and humble, he insisted on calling the town Niplak—Kalpin spelled backward.

It was not a name that felt comfortable on the tongue, but it gave Chig a thrill of pride to say it. "I'm aiming to walk to Niplak," she'd say, never substituting the more common *town*, the way so many people did. "Only a quarter mile left to Niplak," she'd say, crossing the narrow metal bridge put in by the county road crew a few years before her birth. Her father had just started working part-time on the crew then.

Now, with the help of Alberta and a few other girls, Chig shaped her own version of Niplak in soft dirt, as small as it would be if she were a giant looking down from above. Schoolwork was fine, she decided right then and there, but recess couldn't be beat.

Warm days quickly turned the playground dirt into the hard, sunbaked surface God and marble players intended it to be. A bag of marbles, Chig's birthday gift from the Reverend Granddaddy Lukens, sat in her desk, so far unused. Miss Barkus, when asked, suggested that Chig start by learning the rules. "They're sure to have a book for it at the library," she said. "They've got one for everything from making soap to sawing boards from your own trees." (Miss Barkus, Chig guessed, could do both handily.) So Chig put in a request with the library lady when the book wagon made its way from the county seat in Hilltop to Chig's school. And now she spent all her spare minutes paging through a well-worn copy of *Chilter's Official American Marbles Rules and Regulations.* At home, Chig's folks looked to the Bible for answers. That was all well and good, but Chig couldn't remember anything in the Good Book about Jesus or Noah or Moses knuckling down for a game of ringer.

" 'Order of play in a proper game of marbles,' " Chig read aloud after chores, " 'should never be determined by a coin toss or drawing of straws. Players must first lag.' "

Chig paused to lick her lips. She liked the sound of lagging, which according to *Chilter's* involved tossing from something called the taw line. The player whose marble came closer to the opposite lag line got to go first. It was all so orderly and proper.

Chig's fingers twitched. She was ready to move from theory to practice and get down to playing marbles. Right then came a day so sunny and warm Chig's great-aunt was surely thinking the worst. At recess, the scholars spilled out into the schoolyard like so many shiny marbles tipped from a bag. Willy Huddleston sat on a stump, clicking a red-brown aggie and an immie together in his hand. Not having much experience in recess, Chig had never seen him play before. If he attacked marbles with the same energy he put into schoolwork, she figured even a beginner like her stood half a chance. But someone with a longer stride got to Willy first.

"Care to play?" Ed Beemis asked.

"Oh, no, Ed," said Willy, "you wouldn't want to play with someone like me. I'm still learning how to lag."

"Hear that, boys?" Ed called to his friends. "This here Huddleston says he don't know to lag. I thought that's all Huddlestons did know how to do, lag behind everybody else."

It was not a kind thing to say, even if it might be partly true. It brought a roar of laughter from the big boys. Willy tried to act offhand about it.

"Really, Ed," he said, "I'm saving myself."

"Saving yourself?" Ed asked. "For what?"

"I need time to let my skills mature," Willy answered.

"All I see maturing is a coward."

Those were fighting words. Willy shot up from his tree stump. "Who'll lag first?" he asked.

"Not so fast," said Ed. "We need to agree to terms. We'll be playing for keepsies." Willy nodded, and Chig hurried closer. Most games were played for fairsies, not for keepsies. This was serious business. Either Ed or Willy was setting himself up to lose a pile of marbles.

Willy quickly traced the taw and lag lines, a large circle, and an X in the hard dirt. It was just as *Chilter's* had promised: each boy put marbles down on the arms of the

X and prepared to shoot them out of the circle. First, they stood at the taw line. Ed's aggie spun ever so slightly; Willy's landed confidently just short of the lag line. He would go first.

Chuck-ah! Ker-chuck! One after the other, Ed's marbles fell victim to Willy's red-brown aggie.

"Now, just hold on a minute there, Mr. Huddleston!" Ed cried, taking in the extent of the damage. "What kinda rules you playing by?"

"The official rules. *Chilter's.*" Willy boldly clicked a captured mib against another marble in his palm. It wasn't every day that a boy from the small seats at the front of the room beat one of the big boys from the back.

"I think you'd best double-check your copy of *Chilter's,*" Ed said, his brow furrowed in concern. "You've got it all wrong, Willy. Why, if I'm not mistaken, it says right on page fifty-nine that any mib you chuck out like you just done goes instantly and permanently to your opponent."

"'Instantly and permanently,' now, that's a direct quote, ain't it, Ed?" one of the big boys asked.

"Sure is," Ed answered.

"Can't say as I have a copy of *Chilter's* myself," Willy admitted.

"I can see that from the way you play," Ed said. "If you want to know how it's done, just sit back and watch. It's my turn now, anyhow, since you hit a red marble."

Hit a red marble? Chig's eyes bugged out of her head. She had all but memorized page fifty-nine of *Chilter's*—plus the fifty-eight pages before it—and had never read the rules Ed was spouting. If he was cheating, and Chig was pretty sure he was, Ed was going way beyond the usual fudging and histing. "Instantly and permanently" was bad enough, but changing turns based on the color of the marbles was more than she could stomach. Mr. Chilter would be rolling like a marble in his grave if he heard tell.

Wasn't Willy going to protest?

But no. Chig watched as he slowly dropped the aggie and the mibs he'd captured in the dirt, a sure sign of surrender. It was possible he'd never read *Chilter's*. Chig had never seen Willy read anything but the pages Miss Barkus assigned from their readers. And he only half read those.

Chuck-ah! Ker-chuck! The sound of Ed cheating Willy out of marble after marble beat on Chig's ears. Here was injustice, plain and simple. Here was bad sprouting out of good weather, just as her great-aunt had predicted. And yet here was Chig, boots nailed to the ground and mouth clamped shut. Maybe if she were eye level with something higher than Ed's belt buckle and his crisp red bandana, she'd have the courage to say something. She knew she ought to shout out loud. She ought to spring into the center of their game, brandishing her copy of Chilter's and scattering marbles to the four winds.

Chig knew what she ought to do, but getting from ought to do was more than her small self could manage. She watched unblinking as things went from bad to worse. Ed kept his shooter busy until he had captured all but Willy's aggie and a sky blue immie. Willy shrugged as Ed sauntered off to a far corner of the playground, where a group of big boys whooped and hollered. Aggie and immie clicked a few more times in Willy's palm before he dropped them lovingly into the homemade deerskin pouch that lived in his pants pocket. Something in his gesture made Chig, at long last, find her voice.

"Did you know he was cheating you?" Chig whispered. She didn't want to be the one to spread the news that someone had pulled a fast one over poor old Willy Huddleston again. But Willy wouldn't let her pity him.

"Aw, shucks, Chig. Course I knowed it. But you don't think Ed would play with me if he figured I'd win, do you?" Willy tried to smile, but his heart wouldn't let his face do it. The look he gave Chig made her want to cry.

Chig searched for the right thing to say—something just as right and good as Willy's kind words about runts— but she came up blank.

Willy gave his marble bag one last click to fill up

Chig's silence. "Nothing I like better than a good game of marbles," he said. "But in a pinch, a bad one'll do."

"'Spect that's so," Chig said. But her words sounded no more convincing than Willy's. In her heart, she knew that a fellow as decent as Willy shouldn't have to settle for a bad game. If she could somehow find her voice—and the courage to use it—she'd set Ed Beemis straight. In the meantime, she hoped and prayed she could find a way to take the sting out of a heap of lost marbles and a near-empty deerskin pouch.

5

GOOD WORKS

Chig and her family lived half a mile outside Niplak, one of the best excuses for a town in the whole county. Even Chig called it small, but she said it with warmth and sympathy.

Niplak was home to H. J. Gibson's Dry Goods Store, which crowned its main stock of shoes and rugs and other dry goods with smaller lines of hardware (milk cans, harness, and buckets) and groceries (baloney, flour, and eggs). Mr. Gibson liked to say if you couldn't find it in his store, you weren't going to find it anywhere in Niplak, and he was right. His was the only store in town. Across the way stood Floyd Wild's one-room broom factory and

Beemis's Saw and Haul. Closer by was the sorghum mill. At the mill, an ancient mule plodded around and around a worn track while an arm attached to the harness squeezed the life and molasses out of stalks of sorghum. Just before the town center, on a grassy nob of hilltop, stood the Niplak school. Farther down the road a piece, beyond the Saw and Haul, was the Church of Our Redeemer.

One Sunday, the Reverend Argyle Whittle's sermon was on the wonders of good works.

"Yea, though we are but mere humans," he said, pounding a fist on the oaken pulpit, "we need not be like grains of sand on the beach of God's creation."

A grain of sand. Chig had never been to a beach, but she'd seen sand in an hourglass. Each grain looked to be about the size of a chigger—maybe even a little smaller. Chig listened up.

"Let us not be small of heart," the reverend went on, looking somewhere over her head. "Let us remember that good works can make even small men seem tall in the eyes of the Lord."

Chig shivered and squirmed on the bare wooden pew. It wasn't just the way the Reverend Whittle could drag the word Lord out into two syllables. No. It was more that the Lord seemed to be sending a direct order Chig's way. An order not to be small of heart. An order to somehow make up for Willy's lost marbles.

After Sunday service, Chig considered her options. "What do you figure a good work might be, Hubie?"

"Dunno. Maybe helping an old lady carry something or cross the road."

It wasn't much help, but Chig was thankful all the same. During Sunday dinner at noon, her mind was busy, ticking off the names of Niplak's old ladies. The list was fairly short, even including outlying farms and cabins. What was worse, Chig couldn't imagine a one of them needing help carrying something smaller than a log—or crossing a road. Why, most could milk a dozen cows, shuck twenty ears of corn, and stack a cord of firewood without losing a breath. One or two could do all that and blow smoke rings while puffing tobacco in their corncob pipes.

What help could someone as small as Chig offer them?

Days passed, and still she had no notion of how she was going to find the sweet feeling of closeness with the Lord that the Reverend Whittle said came from doing good works. If she couldn't think of something soon, Chig was sure both the reverend and the Lord would be sorely disappointed. Then, on Saturday, her mama saved her.

It was baking day, and Chig was helping settle the round brown loaves on the windowsills and odd corners of wooden countertop to cool.

"Such a shame I can't take a loaf to old Editha Evans," Mama said, shaking her head. "But there's so little time these days for visiting neighborly, what with baby Em."

Chig nodded. Em was sweet, but she sucked up Mama's time like a dry rag on a spill. If Mama couldn't visit neighborly, maybe Chig could do it in her place—and do some good works at the same time. After all, Editha Evans was most definitely an old lady, somewhere close to a hundred years old. And the poor excuse for a road that she lived on might make an able-bodied man happy for an offer of help in crossing it.

"I could take a loaf to her," Chig said. She was already so excited by the very idea that she was hopping from one foot to the other.

Mama raised her eyebrows. "Well, I suppose . . . ," she began. It would be a long walk, even taking the logging path through the woods. Chig couldn't dawdle, coming or going. And she'd have to take care not to get lost.

Chig nodded, her red hair bobbing as she hopped.

Mama tucked a still-warm loaf into a hickory basket and shook her head. "You know Editha doesn't care for children, Chig."

Mama meant it as a warning, but Chig took it as a challenge. Editha was looking more and more like a test of faith. Chig liked tests.

The first mile or two through the woods were easy

going, but soon the brambles thickened. They caught at Chig's ankles and arms. She plunged onward, careful to stay on the trail, a dim outline on the leafy forest floor. She didn't even stop when the sun told her it was lunchtime. She merely pulled out the cold biscuit sandwich Mama had wedged in by the bread and ate while she trudged. She'd need the time to do any spare good works Editha demanded.

Soon enough, Chig was rewarded by the sight of Editha's broken-down cabin. Behind a cloud of tobacco smoke on the porch, she could make out a wooden rocker and the bent form of Editha Evans. When Chig edged closer, she could see that one of Editha's veiny hands held a carved wooden cane—just the thing to use on children, if you didn't much care for them.

"I brought you some bread, Miss Evans," Chig said when she finally caught her breath.

"Whose girl child are you, anyhow?" asked Editha, peering out from her cloud.

"Meg Kalpin's," Chig answered.

"Why, I haven't seen you in years," Editha said, "and I'd put down good money that you haven't grown a bit."

"I'm not shrinking," Chig countered as she stepped onto the creaking wooden porch.

"'Spect that's so." Editha sucked hungrily on her pipe and fingered the loaf of bread. She looked ready to rip into it, but not too ready to share with Chig. From the porch, Chig could see a near-roofless henhouse, but no sign of hens. A gentle clucking from inside the cabin cleared that up. Apparently, Editha had moved her poultry in. Chig knew of lots of folks who were doubling up—young marrieds moving in with parents and in-laws, maiden aunts moving in with sisters and brothers. It happened more and more in these hard times. But Chig had never known someone who doubled up with hens. Here was an old lady who surely needed her help.

"Hey, Miss Evans," Chig said, shifting from one foot to the other, "could I please help you cross the road?"

"What in heaven's name would I want to do that for?" Editha asked. "Nothing over there I can't see from my own porch."

"Well, then," Chig said, looking inside Editha's cabin, "could I give you a hand cleaning up?"

Editha's stick shot out, giving the air near Chig's head a good whack. "Go on and git, girl!" Editha roared. "And tell your mama I'm much obliged for the bread, but I've no need for folks sticking their noses in where they're not needed."

Chig nearly flew off the porch. Who could've known that good works, offered sincerely, might be mistaken for nosiness? She lit on up the path until the woods shut out the sun and any view of Editha Evans's cabin. In the dimness, Chig's shoulders hung so low that the empty basket, light as it was, scraped the ground along the path. The journey that had seemed so quick that morning dragged on the return.

How, Chig wondered, had the early Christians kept from being discouraged? Maybe they'd never run into an Editha Evans. But they must have bumped up against the same kind of problems doing their good works. Had they ever stumbled as badly as Chig? She didn't stop wondering until her basket nearly bounced out of her hand. There, beneath her feet, was a patch of morels—the tastiest wild mushrooms known to humankind. They were ready for the picking.

"Well," said Chig, filling her basket, "all's not lost." She might not be standing any taller in the eyes of the Lord on Sunday, but she was sure to be having a plateful of mushrooms smothered in bacon fat. More than a few folks in Niplak, Chig suspected, would trade the warm feeling one's soul got from good works for a mess of warm morels in springtime.

Mama saved three wrinkly brown slivers of mushroom from the skillet just so she could call them leftovers and put them on top of the slice of baloney in Chig's sandwich. Chig snuck a hungry peek or two at the slivers during pauses in Monday morning's lessons at school. At lunchtime, Willy leaned against the sycamore where Chig sat eating and shot a whisper. "Where'd you find them, Chig?"

Chig was dumbstruck. Here was her chance at last to do a truly good work and make it up to Willy. But she couldn't say a word. How could she? Nobody in Niplak would divulge the location of a patch of morels to any but a blood relation. Secrets like that were sacred. More than one too-chatty son or daughter had been banished from ever setting foot in the family cabin for leaking the location of a good morel patch. Morels were more precious and rare than cash money around Niplak.

Chig gave Willy a mournful stare, but he just laughed.

"Don't you worry, Chig," he said. "I understand. Not that your secret wouldn't be safe with me, if you should change your mind."

Another good work botched. Chig hoped the good Lord wasn't counting. She tried to make it up to Willy by asking politely about how many morels he'd found so far that spring. But she stopped when Ed Beemis sidled up to the tree.

"Care for a game of marbles, Willy?" Ed's smile was oily and greedy enough to turn a stomach full of baloney-and-mushroom sandwich. But this time, Chig was determined not to let a little queasiness get between her and speaking out. She stood as tall as she could, already imagining herself quoting—word for word—the rules from Chilter's. But Willy stopped her cold.

"Sorry, Ed," he said. "Gave it up for Lent."

"For Lent?" Ed asked. "Couldn't you have given up something normal, like chocolate?"

"Gave that up too," Willy answered. "Might even keep it up *after* Lent."

Ed was a regular attender at the Church of Our Redeemer. Getting religion raised Willy a notch or two in his eyes. Ed sauntered off, looking for easier pickings. Pickings who weren't on such good terms with the Lord.

"Did you really give up marbles and chocolate?" Chig asked. She had never known anyone to make such a sacrifice.

"In a way, Chig," Willy answered. "I'd done made up my mind to give up chocolate, but darned if I didn't want to at least taste it again before I'd give it up. So I traded my aggie and my immie to Georgie Gibson for two Hershey bars."

"But how could you trade away your last marbles?"

"Ever eaten too much of your favorite food and then thrown it up?" Willy asked.

"Nope," Chig answered, confused.

"Well," said Willy, "if you ever do, you'll know that

after that, you can't even look at your favorite food without it giving you a sour stomach. My stomach needs a rest from marbles, and next to marbles, a Hershey bar might just be my favorite thing."

Chig remembered how her stomach had felt that first time Ed Beemis had called her a runt, and how it still rumbled sometimes when the big boys slapped and scratched at their play chigger bites. Wasn't there something she could do to settle Willy's stomach? Maybe if he could play a game or two of marbles where he was sure to win, fair and square, he'd get his taste for it back.

"Want to help me work on my shooting . . . after Lent, I mean?" Chig asked.

"I might be persuaded," said Willy.

Chig feared she would never stand any taller in the eyes of the Lord, but with Willy's help, she stood a good chance of turning into a mean hand at marbles.

6

CHANDU SUMMER

That summer, well after the end of Lent and Chig's ninth birthday, Willy became Chig's teacher. He regularly gave lessons in the schoolyard or in the hard dirt of the drive leading up to the Kalpin home. He was a deft coach, throwing only a few words of carefully chosen advice—and a few marbles—Chig's way. Slowly but surely, she learned to lag and knuckle down.

Toward summer's end, Chig played her best game yet. She managed to win two marbles from Willy, although since all the marbles were hers and they always ended up in her pouch, it was hard to say who won what. Em sat clapping in the grass by the drive, and Hubie watched from his usual perch high in the branches of a shade tree.

That evening after supper Chig still basked in the glow of capturing marbles, while Hubie stayed close by her side on the kitchen bench. Even though he was brave enough to climb anything, Hubie was scared of some things. A windstorm sputtered and raged outside. It pressed against the windowpanes, causing them to rattle. Gusts made the flame in the kerosene lantern dance. But Chig knew this wasn't the source of Hubie's unease.

Over the sounds of the storm, the two of them were listening to an announcer's deep and mysterious voice. Chig could feel the fear in Hubie's ragged breath each time the announcer spoke. That voice always marked the beginning of Chig's favorite radio show, *Chandu the Magician*. Chandu, born plain vanilla Frank Chandler in the U.S. of A., had learned the secrets of the ancients from a yogi in India. Now he used his magical powers to serve as a secret agent fighting evil for the American government. Evil, Chig found, tended to be in faraway places, like Istanbul or Shanghai. But wherever it was, Frank Chandler rooted it out and fought back, sometimes conferring with his crystal ball. His enemy was named Roxor.

"Isn't that Roxor just a hundred and ten percent pure evil?" Hubie asked, nudging closer.

"Can't nothing be more than a hundred percent

anything," Chig answered. "But I know what you mean. I wouldn't want to meet Roxor in the woods behind Niplak."

Radio was Chig's favorite kind of entertainment. She'd seen a moving picture once in Indianapolis, and it was fine and dandy. But radio shows didn't overwhelm your eyes. They left the seeing to the imagination. Shows like *Chandu* spent more time describing scenes—"a dusty street in Cairo's native quarter"—than they did describing people. Chig could close her eyes and see Frank Chandler any way she pleased. In her mind, he was small, but well proportioned. Plain, but in a pleasing, almost handsome way. A sturdy fellow made extraordinary by his magical powers.

Always somewhere near the beginning of the show, never where you could predict for sure, came the announcer's cry *"Chaaaan-duuu the Magician!"*, followed by the sound of a gong struck hard enough to raise the ancients from their graves. Hubie nearly leaped out of his skin.

"Ooh-wee," he explained, swiping an arm around, "my back itches!" Then he sat again, pressed close to Chig.

"Shhh," Chig said. Why did Hubie think he had to be brave for her, anyway? But this time, the crash of the gong was followed by a louder, even more ominous cracking and hissing. Hubie grabbed Chig's arm and gave her a wordless, wild stare.

"What on earth?" Chig asked.

"The cherry," Mama answered from the kitchen, where she was peering out the window. Chig knew there was a large, thick old cherry tree not twenty-five yards from the Kalpin home. From the thumps that followed the cracking and hissing, Chig figured the cherry tree was no more.

"Lucky it didn't hit the house or the barn," Daddy said when he came back from a quick inspection. The wind was quieting, and after the latest episode of *Chandu* ended, Chig could hear her parents talking about the tree.

"It'd bring at least fifty dollars, Meg," Daddy was saying, "if we had it cut into paneling and sold it at the Saw and Haul."

"But Curtis," Mama said, "I thought we agreed we'd use that tree to panel our own house someday."

Chig glanced at the room around her, with its painted fiberboard walls. She'd always liked the unfinished look of their house, the way it was a work in progress, with Daddy remodeling bits of the place at a time. But she could imagine how warm, red cherry would finish off the family's kitchen and front room in a high-tone way.

"I know what we agreed," Daddy said, "but we've got lots of extras to pay for these days."

"Yep," Mama said.

Chig thought of the new school shoes she'd been begging for. She thought of the doctor's bill for the gash Hubie had put into his leg when he'd jumped out of a tree and hit a sharp rock. And she thought of how baby Em wore out her clothes scooting on her behind across the ground. (She resolutely refused to crawl as other babies did. Chig admired her stubbornness.)

"Fifty dollars would buy lots of extras," Daddy said, and that was the end of the conversation.

The next morning, the sun rose bright and warm, drying up the sogginess left by the storm. Instead of playing ringer, Chig and Willy helped Mr. Kalpin gather fallen branches and stack firewood. The tree was twisted by the wind, broken into two main chunks of trunk. Everyone but Em pitched in to load the chunks onto the bed of the Model A. Chig and Willy pulled themselves onto the high bench seat in the cab. A trip to Beemis's Saw and Haul—and the promise of hearing grown-up talk about the night's storm—was so tempting, the two decided marbles could wait. Chig never stopped to think that Ed might be helping out, but there he was perched on a stool in the office.

Ed's dad and Chig's daddy headed out to the truck to start the process of milling the wood into boards. Chig and Willy tried to follow, but Ed was off his stool in a flash, blocking the way out of the cramped office.

"What brings you two together," he asked, "so far from the kiddie row at school?"

"I'm teaching Chig how to play marbles," Willy said.

"Thought you gave 'em up."

"Only for Lent, Ed," Willy said. "The Spirit led me back to the game this summer."

Ed looked skeptical.

"So now you're training up Chig to play me?" he asked.

"To beat you, more like," Willy answered. "She's a fine player."

Chig gulped, and Ed gasped.

"Beat me? You lost all but two of your marbles in our last game. How could any student of yours hope to beat me?"

"In a game played fair and square, by the rules," Willy said, "any decent player could beat you, Ed Beemis."

Chig liked the way Willy said "decent," but she wasn't so sure she liked the way the conversation was headed.

"'Fair and square'? 'By the rules'? What's that you're saying, Willy Huddleston?" Only the saw screamed louder than Ed.

"He's saying the truth, that's what." Chig whispered, not expecting to be heard, but the saw came to the end of a log and abruptly stopped its screaming. Chig's words dropped into a moment of pure silence, like rain falling on the still surface of a pool of water.

Ed pulled out his red bandana and looked ready to

swat Chig with it. But suddenly the office door flew open. Mr. Beemis blew in. He was a large and powerful man who moved in quick, efficient bursts. "You got that receipt totaled up, Ed?" he asked.

Ed didn't. Hadn't had time. Now, instead of swatting at Chig, he was swabbing his red bandana on his sweaty face, trying to figure fast. Ed's face grew as red as his hanky.

Willy nodded to Chig. The path to the door was clear, and it seemed like a good time to leave. They waited in the truck cab for Mr. Kalpin.

"Willy Huddleston," Chig said, "now we're both in it deep for sure."

"Yep."

"Ed Beemis may not be the best player in the world— if you're playing fair and square—but he's sure better than I am."

"Now, maybe," said Willy with a smile. "The summer's still young."

It wasn't that young. There were only a few weeks left before school. When Chig met up with Ed Beemis for a game of ringer, she'd need magical powers the size of Frank Chandler's to win.

7

CHIG LEARNS A NEW, OLD ADDRESS

When school started and Chig walked by the back row of seats, Ed Beemis's steady, hard gaze cut through her like a saw blade slicing a log. Summer had turned to a wet, chill fall. Although at times Chig longed for warmer days and a game of ringer, she felt a certain relief when, day after day, it was too soggy in the schoolyard for rolling aggies and immies.

The days grew colder, and Miss Barkus threw heavy work shirts on over her shapeless black dresses for warmth. Chig's mama wrapped a hand-knit scarf around her older daughter's neck. Even the shortest scarf in the cedar chest wrapped several times around Chig, making it hard for her to move her head much. Mama had done such a thorough job of tucking in the ends, and the schoolhouse was so chilly, that Chig was still wearing the scarf when Miss Barkus introduced the week's recitation one Monday morning.

"Scholars," she said, tapping her pointer on the chalkboard, "we are going to learn the Gettysburg Address.

"I expect," she went on, "for you to do your level best this week to memorize as much as you can of President Lincoln's fine address. But I do allow that some of our smallest scholars may not be up to committing the whole thing to memory."

Chig's nose itched, but for once she forgot to scratch. Recitation was her strong suit. She was good at memorizing the short poems and sayings Miss Barkus usually assigned to the younger students. Her curiosity overcoming her, Chig turned to Willy and whispered, "How long can a Gettysburg address be? Longer than a rural route?"

Willy, who had been held back on account of laziness, set Chig straight. "It's more like a sermon," he told her. "Don't know why they call it an address. And make no mistake, Chig, this thing's longer than a rural route." His eyes wandered to the big board. There, for the first time, Chig focused on what lay beneath Miss Barkus's pointer— a vast sea of words.

Chig gulped hard, scratched her nose, and settled in to

get her feet wet. Miss Barkus tried to make things easier for her scholars. "Imagine, if you will, a battlefield where the corpses of men and horses lie buried none too deep in the ground. Imagine a November morning when the scent of death still lingers in the air."

A shiver passed over the room. Chig sniffed the morning air and thought she caught the scent. Who hadn't, while rambling in the woods, stumbled upon the rotting carcass of an old doe, left half eaten by the dogs and coyotes? Who among them hadn't helped their daddy drag an old cow or a goat—one that had the poor manners to die of disease and not be fit for eating—to the back forty for burial? Once she could smell the Gettysburg Address, Chig found it was a whole lot easier to commit it to memory. Not that it wasn't hard work, her coaching Willy, and Willy doing his best to coach her. But the scent of death helped her paint a picture in her mind. Slowly, the words fit into the picture.

On Thursday, Miss Barkus's oldest and most seasoned scholars began the parade up to the front of the room. There, backs to the chalkboard, they recited as much as they could from memory. Daisy Settle, Doc Settle's youngest and the first to go, choked a bit upon the opening words so they came out sounding a bit like "Foot sores and seven ears ago." Otherwise, Chig thought, she did a lovely job.

Even Ed Beemis did all right. He had, after all, been reading the scripture lessons to the congregation at the

Church of Our Redeemer since he was as young as Chig. All that experience served him well, although he had trouble with "the last full measure of devotion." It got turned into "the vast-full pleasure of devotion." Chig liked the sound of a word like *vast-full*, but Miss Barkus, being a stickler for precision, marked him down for it.

With each successive recitation that afternoon and the next, Chig's lips moved along with the scholar's. When they stumbled, she did not. And it wasn't that she was reading the words on the board as they spoke. Chig had nailed this one. Cold.

By late Friday afternoon, when the littlest and laziest scholars—the ones in Chig and Willy's row—were called to the front, Chig was more than ready. She was near to bursting with the pressure of Lincoln's words, packed tight in her brain and trying like mad to escape out her mouth.

She managed to stay seated during Willy's recitation only by anchoring her feet around the wrought-iron legs of her desk—still the smallest in the schoolroom.

" 'Four score and seven years ago, our fathers brought forth upon this continent, a new nation . . .' " It was a glorious beginning for someone who hadn't gotten beyond "Four score" before.

" 'A new nation . . .', " he said again, then stopped. Snickers could be heard from the back row, but Miss Barkus smiled and nodded encouragingly at Willy.

That broke the spell.

Never in his years of half trying and quarter listening to lessons had Willy Huddleston deserved both a smile and an encouraging nod from his teacher. It was too much for him. He couldn't go on.

Not that Miss Barkus hadn't done her level best to get Willy to learn. But even she had her limits. "You can lead a horse to water," she'd say, "but you can't make him drink." She did what she could to make learning appealing to a horse like Willy, but she couldn't force him into the creek.

Under Chig's coaching, Willy had almost seemed thirsty enough to put his mouth to the water trough of learning. But that possibility vanished in an instant. Willy smiled and nodded back to his teacher before sliding into his seat.

"Chig Kalpin!" Miss Barkus barked. "Next!"

Chig sprang up like a red flag on a mailbox ready to tell the world about all the learning stored inside her. Even the hair on her head seemed to stand on end, making her look taller than usual. Her boots barely touched the ground when she walked to the front of the class. Balanced on tiptoe, hands clenched behind her, she dove right in: " '. . . a new nation, conceived in Liberty, and dedicated to the proposition that all men are created equal.' " One paragraph down; two to go.

" 'We have come to dedicate a portion of it, as a final resting place . . .' " Chig chugged through the second paragraph with ease. She was building steam as she made her way to the last and longest part of Lincoln's address.

"'. . . We cannot dedicate, we cannot consecrate, we cannot hallow, this ground. The brave men, living and dead, who struggled here . . .'" A stiff northerly breeze shot through the crack under the front door and came to a stop at Chig's nose. There it was again, stronger now. The scent of death. Smelled like somebody had been slaughtering hogs.

In that breeze, Chig caught again a hint of what folks had smelled while gathered on a long-ago battlefield. The words she was saying were more than just words. Chig could feel what they might have meant to the people who had heard them for the first time that November day. They felt like a prayer for a wounded nation. A prayer from a man who surely stood tall in the eyes of the Lord.

Chig faltered, then began again. "'The brave men, living and dead, who struggled . . .'"

Snort!

Chig wasn't the only person to find inspiration in the stench of a dead hog. Ed Beemis's snorts and grunts continued. Behind his red bandana they could be mistaken for a bad cold. Miss Barkus must have thought so, but Chig wasn't fooled. She knew full well what Ed meant to say.

Runt.

The word stopped her recitation cold. Fear draped over her. She saw before her a sunny spring day to come, with schoolyard dirt hardened to perfection and Ed challenging her to a game of ringer. The Gettysburg Address seemed small and insignificant in comparison, just as Chig felt. Even Miss Barkus's most encouraging nods and smiles couldn't restart Chig. She clumped down from her tiptoes and dragged herself back to her seat.

In the kitchen window the kerosene lamp shone golden and bright, already lit as Chig trudged home from school under a darkening sky. Mama wiped the flour on her apron before she took Chig's narrow chin in her hands and peered down.

"You all right, Chig?" she asked. It was Mama's normal evening greeting.

"Guess so," Chig answered. If Mama heard some of Chig's anguish, she didn't say. Instead, she nudged her toward Hubie, who had been asking for a reading from *Illustrated Stories from the Bible* for some time, to no avail. Em took wavering steps across the floor and lunged onto Chig's lap. Hubie plopped down next to them on the front room's braided rug. He leaned over his little big sister's shoulder to get a closer look at the pictures. Even out of the steamy kitchen and far from the stove, Chig began to feel warm inside.

At table, Daddy asked Chig to say grace. Usually the smell of Mama's cooking ensured that any blessing was short and sweet. This night was different.

"Thanks for the food, Lord," Chig began, "and will you please listen in again after we're done eating? I'll have more to say then. Amen."

Daddy's big bushy eyebrows bobbed, but he didn't question the blessing. Mama kept quiet, as usual. Hubie was too busy sniffing hot buttered corn bread to hear what Chig had said anyway. Everyone, including baby Em listened up, though, when supper was over.

Chig tucked the last of the corn bread crumbs into her mouth, finished off her jar of milk, and stood up on the bench she shared with Hubie. She looked down from her high vantage point and saw warm, well-fed, and expectant faces—not a snorter among them.

"I will now recite the Gettysburg Address," Chig began. "Although considering it's an address, it's pretty long, and I'll only say the whole thing if you think you've got the time."

"Plenty of time," Daddy said, and Mama smiled. Hubie didn't have a say in it. Em gnawed furiously on her corn bread.

"Ahem. Well. It was four score and seven years ago," Chig began. She didn't stop until she got to "this nation, shall have a new birth of freedom—and that government of the people, by the people, for the people, shall not perish from the earth."

Her daddy, who'd been through the same one-room school, was ready to give Chig a word or a hint here and there. She never needed his help. Her mother, who'd gone to inferior city schools, looked on in amazement. She gathered up a corner of her flour-whitened apron to dab a tear from her eye.

If Chig hadn't finished her chores in the henhouse quite so fast, she never would have heard what her parents had to say about the Gettysburg Address. But when she pulled open the screen and nudged the side door with her knee, her folks were both at the dry sink, backs to her. "Too bad the Federals couldn't have won," Daddy said, "but Lincoln wrote a mighty fine address just the same."

"I reckon so," Mama answered, but Daddy went on as if he hadn't even heard her.

"And Lincoln couldn't have done a finer job of saying it than our Chig."

"No indeed," said Mama.

Chig pulled back her knee, nice and quiet, and stood on the porch. She drank in the cool night air. Even the coolness couldn't make her color fade. Chig glowed the warm, bright red of a chigger bite, but felt none of the sting, none of the swelling, and none of the itch.

8

FAMILY

The next several weeks were a blur of busyness, and that was a blessing. Folks with much stronger constitutions than Chig's had been known to lose all sense of proportion after hearing the kind of praise she'd chanced on at the porch door.

Chig's color faded as she slipped into the rhythm of more ordinary days. In spare moments at school, she tried to give Willy words of encouragement, to help him share in the warmth.

"Your Gettysburg Address was pretty long," she said.

"Only 'cause you helped me. I never got so far before on my own."

"Hey," said Chig, "you know I owe you. I'd never have learned marbles so fast just reading *Chilter's* on my own."

Willy was silent at first. "Come spring," he said finally, "we'll get back to our lessons. And maybe by then you'll have grown an inch or two. Your shooting arm could use just a tad more length to match up to Ed's."

Chig blinked. Since that talk about runts so long ago, Willy had never mentioned her size in so many words. He'd shown a certain delicacy that way, and she'd always appreciated it. Chig could tell he meant well by what he said now. But it scared the daylights out of her. Her mama and daddy had been encouraging her to grow for years, and they hadn't had much effect. She was still as petite as could be. Would Willy's encouragement do any better? And if she didn't grow, how could she ever hope to beat Ed Beemis at marbles?

Chig was relieved when school finally let out for the holidays. This year the holidays would be extra special because Chig's aunt Dorothea was visiting. She planned to ride down with Doc and Mrs. Settle, who liked to do their Christmas shopping in Indianapolis. With times being hard, the Settles returned with fewer and fewer packages each year. But they always carried home thrilling descriptions of the window displays and the top-floor tearoom at the L. S. Ayres department store. As second cousins of

Chig's daddy's mama, the Settles were more than happy to give Aunt Dorothea a ride in their 1927 Pierce-Arrow.

Aunt Dorothea was a dietitian. "That's someone who loves to eat but can't cook," Chig had guessed once when Hubie asked. She'd been more than half right. Later, Chig learned that Dorothea was on the staff of the Indianapolis Children's Hospital and that she even got paid for what she did. "She tells the cooks what to fix," Chig explained, and Hubie nodded.

Unlike every other woman—and most of the men—in Chig's family, Aunt Dorothea didn't care to cook, even at home. But she didn't let that stop her from bringing food along when she visited. What kind of company wouldn't bring something tasty for the host? Pressing down on her lap over the fifty-mile trip from Indianapolis was a cardboard box filled with exotic canned goods. These were the kind that came in metal, direct from the shelves of a grocery store, not in glass jars like the ones stored in Chig's mama's root cellar.

Chig helped her aunt unpack the box onto the kitchen table late the Friday before Christmas. "My land," said Chig. She traced the outline of a fish struggling on a line with her chewed-down fingernail. The cans' printed labels promised lush purple plums in syrup, Packt Fresh beets, salmon from Washington state, and even deviled ham.

"Oh, Dorothea, you shouldn't have," Mama told her sister. She looked almost ready to cry at the bounty set out before her.

"Meg," Dorothea said, "don't think it! Don't think for a minute that I'm trying to say your cooking isn't up to par. Don't we both know for a certainty that's how you landed such a fine husband?"

Dorothea winked at Chig. "Don't make my mistake, girlie," she said, leaning down close. "I can barely boil an egg, and look where I am now. Thirty-one and an old maid!"

"But you don't look like the maid in the deck," Chig said. She played Old Maid sometimes on Sundays with her Kalpin cousins. Daddy's brother Elwin's boys had a set of the cards. In that deck, the old maid was the saddest, homeliest, tiredest-looking woman you ever chanced to see.

Chig thought Dorothea looked grand in her flowered dress and smart, citified wool coat. She meant to say so, but Aunt Dorothea's conversation had rolled on by her. Chig listened to the lilt in her aunt's voice. It hinted that boiled eggs could be quite tasty and that perhaps the life of an old maid held its own charms.

Soon the natural disruption of having a houseguest settled into a more or less comfortable pattern. "Hubie, you sleep here," Mama had said that first night, pointing to the padded armchair in the front room. And so the children's room was magically turned into the "girls'" room for the two weeks of Aunt Dorothea's visit.

Churchgoing and visiting neighborly on the first Sunday of Aunt Dorothea's stay involved a few adjustments. She was not overlarge but took up a full adult amount of space in the Model A. Em balanced on Dorothea's lap in the middle of the seat, with Mrs. Kalpin squished in by the door. Chig and Hubie bundled up extra warm, scarves around their necks and faces. Then Daddy tied them in place just behind the cab in the rough wooden truck bed.

At Chig's grandfolks' after church, the big oak table was set for the noonday meal, but not before two of the stronger boy cousins had fit in the leaf. Chig found a vast expanse covered with good china, heavy silver cutlery (not all of which matched), and a linen table runner topped with a centerpiece of fake fruit and pine boughs to celebrate the last Sunday before Christmas. Oh, the grandness of it all!

"Dare you to take a bite out of that pear," Cora said. She was one of Chig's cousins from Kentucky, visiting for the holidays.

"It's made out of wax, Cora," Chig said. "You got me to bite the banana when I was five."

"How old are you now?" Cora asked, looking Chig up and down.

"Nine."

"Well, don't that beat all," said Cora. "Don't that beat all."

Chig stood straighter and moved on to the kitchen.

"Set the corn bread and biscuits over on that board, Edna," said Granny Shorty Kalpin. She nearly had to shout to be heard over the din. Mama and the other women were busy carting in pans of corn bread, still-warm buttermilk biscuits, kettles heavy with limas and turnips, and cooked peeled potatoes ready for mashing with generous dollops of cream. Even Aunt Dorothea was working hard to free beets from two large metal cans. They were all so busy that not a one of them noticed Chig. Hubie grabbed their attention instead.

"Mama!" he said, his voice oddly muffled. "Cousin Cora made me eat wax!"

Mama took his chin in her hand, gently scraped his front teeth clean, and sent him on his way. A chorus of aunts giggled after him, and Granny Shorty slapped her thigh. Then she pulled a ham from the biggest chamber of her stove and stumbled backward.

"Lord have mercy. What was that small, bony thing I hit?" Granny asked when she got her balance back.

"Chig" came the answer from a heap of Sunday dress and frizzy hair.

"Watch your toes, girl!" said Granny, helping Chig up. "Hate to say it, but you take more after me every time I see you."

"Yep."

"Not a whole lot bigger than the turkey I've got warming in my side oven," said Granny. It was a substantial turkey, but Chig still winced at the comparison. She might be small, but she knew she was bigger than the main course at Sunday dinner.

"Now, if you don't want Grandpa to start carving you up by mistake," Granny went on, "you'd better hightail it out of my kitchen."

Chig spotted Grandpa Kalpin on the back porch sharpening his blade, so she ducked into the parlor. She managed to steer clear of carving knives and other trouble until dinnertime. Then all the grandfolks, aunts and uncles, and cousins from near and far pulled chairs up around the table. Surely family—particularly a family so well stocked with good cooks—should be a blessing. Yet with her hands folded in a tent beneath her nose, Chig said "Amen" without enthusiasm.

Just that Friday the library lady had come to Chig's school. She'd delivered—as requested—a book whose mud-brown cloth cover promised to reveal the secrets of *Modern Nutrition for Growth*. Chig had plowed a path through the dense field of words only as far as page five. But even at that early stage in her reading, she could tell that modern nutrition looked down upon plump turkeys, fat hams, and sweet pumpkin pies.

"Iron," Chig read, "will produce excellent results when ingested in quantity among juveniles." That meant, near as Chig could make out, no turkey, no ham, and certainly no pie. As each heaping platter rounded the table, Chig breathed deeply but did not fork or spoon over her usual hefty portions. Her plate stayed bare. Soon even the sight of the wax pears was causing her stomach to growl.

Finally, after most folks had started eating, Daddy took note.

"Feeling poorly, Chig?" he asked.

"Nope," Chig answered.

"Had too much cornmeal mush for breakfast?" Granny Shorty asked.

"Nope."

"You're not on a diet, let's hope."

"No, ma'am," Chig told her granny. "Just haven't seen anything that I'd like to eat."

"Are you blind, child?" Grandpa Kalpin roared. Picky eaters had no business sitting at his table.

Granny Shorty shot her husband a calming glance, then turned back to Chig.

"A body needs food, Chig," she said, "even a small one like yours or mine. Now, what do you reckon you'd like to eat?"

"I might fancy some liver. And maybe a small bowlful of blackstrap molasses," she said.

"Liver!" cried Grandpa in disgust.

"What's the molasses for, Chig?" Cousin Cora whispered. "Dipping?"

Chig's mama nearly choked on a mouthful of stuffing. She looked ready to spring up and slap a wrist on Chig's forehead to check for a temperature.

Granny Shorty shushed them all.

"Why liver and molasses," she asked, "when we got so much of the good Lord's bounty right here on the table?"

"They're excellent sources of iron," Chig answered.

"Is that so?" Granny said.

"They certainly are." Aunt Dorothea's voice was strong and confident. It was the voice of someone who knew a thing or two about iron and, quite possibly, about modern nutrition.

"We could all use some iron," she went on, turning to Chig. "But what exactly do you want so much for?"

"It's supposed to help you grow." Chig stared at her reflection on her plate. She felt too small, just then, to meet Aunt Dorothea's eyes.

"Well," said Dorothea, "if it's growing you want to do, you came to the right table."

Chig looked up, astonished.

"Sure, Chig," her aunt went on. "Liver and molasses aren't the only good growing foods." There was, Chig discovered, iron beyond imagining right inside the slightly chipped covered dish that held Granny Shorty's creamed spinach. Heaps of things called protein and calcium lay hidden in juicy hams, buttery limas, pecan pies, and cottage cheese. Even Aunt Ida's bread-and-butter pickles were revealed to be wonderfully healthy as well as crisp and tangy. "I've read," Dorothea said, "that the vinegar in pickle brine will help your hair grow." Mama's corn bread stuffing was full of something called carbohydrates; they sounded so good for growing that Chig took an extra-large portion when the platter passed by her again.

Chig's stomach was still full that night when she and Aunt Dorothea snuggled into bed. Baby Em's satisfied snores and snuffles could be heard from the crib in the corner. Chig reached to turn down the wick on the kerosene lantern when Dorothea shook her head.

"Let's just lie and chat awhile," she said.

Chig didn't mind. The lantern cast a mellow glow on the walls and ceilings. It made the room seem warmer than it really was. "Mighty fine dinner today," she said.

"More than fine, Chig," said Aunt Dorothea. "Good to see you eating so well."

"You figure if I keep on eating all those growing foods, I'll have a spurt?" Chig asked.

"It could happen," Aunt Dorothea answered. "And anyway, it sure can't hurt."

Chig blinked. What had seemed so certain over dinner now sounded like an untested theory of modern nutrition.

"Make no mistake, Chig. If you eat well, you're bound to grow as much as your body was meant to. But we're not all meant to be big."

Chig gulped hard, hoping to keep the tears at bay. Her aunt didn't seem to notice.

"If I were you, girlie, I'd heap my plate high and look for some shoes with heels, just to be on the safe side. After all, you don't want to be invisible, do you?"

Invisible? Chig had no idea what her aunt was on about now. Not even Chandu the Magician had the power to become invisible.

"You know, Chig, to be small or to be quiet on its own is no great disability in life. But if you're both at once, you're apt to be invisible. . . ."

That word, invisible, caught Chig up so she barely heard the rest. She looked down at her hands, her fingers spread from habit to touch the small, soft snippets of velvet on the crazy quilt. Clearly she hadn't become invisible yet.

But maybe you couldn't trust your eyes in a case like this. Chig snuck a hand up the sleeve of her nightgown and pinched herself. Hard. It hurt enough to convince her she was still there.

"Course, maybe you *want* to be invisible," Aunt Dorothea went on. "I knew a shy girl once who used to dream that if she stayed quiet enough and crossed her fingers hard enough, nobody'd notice her a-tall."

"Did it work?" Chig asked. She kept her own fingers resolutely uncrossed.

"No, it did not. Plus, turned out there were plenty of times with plenty of people when she figured she'd just as soon notice and be noticed."

Chig gave Dorothea a sidelong glance. It was hard to see the little girl she might once have been in that grown-up face and in the calm hands spread over the quilt, but maybe Aunt Dorothea had crossed her fingers a time or two when she was young. Chig didn't want to let on that she knew who her aunt was talking about.

"That so?" she asked.

"Mm-hmm," Aunt Dorothea answered. "Sweet dreams, Chig. Sweet dreams." She turned down the wick. The soft glow faded quickly into a chill darkness. Breaths soon came regular and deep—all but Chig's

"Night, Aunt Dorothea," she whispered.

A few weeks later, after Christmas stockings had been emptied and Aunt Dorothea had gone back to her job

telling cooks what to feed sick children, Chig found herself alone with her father in the barn.

"Am I too quiet, Daddy?" she asked. Her small but strong fingers urged milk to flow from Bossie, the family's best-natured cow. Daddy took charge of the more reluctant udders.

"Can't say that I've noticed," Daddy said. The pinging of warm milk sounded in the bucket between his feet. "But come to think of it, some folks have said a word or two to me along those lines."

"Honest?" asked Chig.

"Well," said Daddy, "I don't recall exactly. But I'd allow as how to some folks—specially from out of county—you'd seem a mite quiet."

This didn't sound good. Chig just hoped it wasn't getting any worse.

"On the level, Daddy," Chig said, "will I ever get any bigger'n I am now?"

"On the level?" Daddy asked.

"Yep. I'm ready for the truth."

Daddy paused in his milking. In the silence, Chig fidgeted. Had she finally found a question he couldn't answer?

No. Not hardly.

"Course you're going to grow, Chig. Without a doubt."

Chig had only gotten partway through a sigh of relief when her daddy went on.

"Now, you're very nearly as tall as Granny Shorty already, so it's hard to say how much more you'll sprout. But there's all kinds of growing a body can do," he said, patting his cow's rough side to keep her calm. "You've got a big heart, Chig, and near as I can tell it's getting bigger every day. That brain of yours is growing, too. One of these days, the rest of you is bound to catch up, leastways a little bit."

Daddy didn't hold out much promise, but Chig grabbed on to it all the same. She needed hope, a good appetite, and a lot of luck, she figured, if she was going to keep from going invisible—and grow into the big person she meant to be.

9

SPRING 1935

Spring came early the year Chig turned ten. By mid-February, balmy southern breezes were eating away at the last forlorn patches of snow. Chig still hadn't had a spurt, and yet it seemed that all the world around her was growing. Grass, surprised to be wakened early from its winter sleep, shot up and managed to look respectably green. Leaf buds poked out at the tips of tree branches. Even baby Em sprouted in the warmth. She now wore a dress Chig remembered getting for her fourth birthday. Sure, Mama had hemmed it, but Chig was still shocked to see it hanging on a one-year-old.

Just after mid-March, Miss Barkus confirmed that

spring had come for good. Refusing all volunteers, she stood on the steps, personally whacking the dirty erasers together. She gazed off through a chalk-dust haze at the dogwood and the redbud trees. Finally, on one particularly warm day, she had Willy open the windows a crack.

The breeze that came in smelled of moss. It hinted at good mushroom hunting—and frying and eating—in the days ahead. It lifted the pages of Chig's reader. Having already finished her assignment, Chig read ahead, wherever the wind chose to take her.

She was so intent she didn't noticed that Miss Barkus had written the date March 21, 1935, in her fine script upon the chalkboard. Now Chig's teacher was tapping with her pointer. "Scholars," she asked, "what important event will occur on this date?"

Perhaps the warm air made her classmates more sluggish than usual. Chig looked around uneasily. No one raised a hand. One or two of them at least must have known the answer. They always had in the past. Sometimes, Chig knew, Teacher would offer clues to nudge her scholars in the right direction. That seemed unlikely to happen today. Something about Miss Barkus's tapping said she expected to hear the right answer—and soon.

Miss Barkus's best scholars, plus a wise apple or two, soon raised their hands in the air. Chig sat back in relief when Daisy Settle was called on to answer. Daisy planned to become a schoolteacher, just like Miss Barkus. She even hoped to go to the Hilltop Academy next year "to further her education," as she put it.

But sometimes, even Daisy failed.

"No, Daisy," Miss Barkus said, "it is not the date upon which the swallows return to San Juan Capistrano in California."

Chig saw Daisy's shoulders sag under the sorrow of it all.

Willy tried next. Chig had no idea where he found the energy to raise his hand and wave it about so wildly. Spring must have gone straight to his head.

"Is it Stan Laurel's birthday?" Willy asked.

Miss Barkus brought her pointer around sharply to stop the hoots of laughter seeping out of the back row. She looked as if she'd have whacked a head or two if Ed and his buddies had been within pointer range. Chig even wondered if she meant to whack Willy, but she must have heard the genuine interest in his voice.

"I am not certain of the comic actor's birthday, Willy, but I will endeavor to find out. In the meantime, let me remind scholars of the question: What important event will occur on this date?"

"Guess that wasn't it," mumbled Willy as he settled back into his customary laziness.

Chig was mightily concerned. She was pretty sure she

knew the answer. March 21 was her aunt Verna's birthday. Verna was her daddy's oldest sister. She'd helped Granny Shorty raise Daddy and Elwin and the other Kalpin children. Verna had a near and dear place in Chig's daddy's heart. And it just so happened that she was named after the vernal equinox.

Chig's daddy had explained it to her two springs ago, when the equinox had fallen a day shy of Aunt Verna's birthday. They had just finished their chores in the barn. Chig was trying hard not to spill any of the warm, fresh milk from her pail.

"Red sky at night . . . ," Daddy began, pointing upward.

And Chig whispered the ending, "Sailor's delight." It was a sunset so large and deep and lovely that it nearly took her breath away.

"How did the sun get to be as big as it is?" Chig asked at last.

"Dunno, Chig. But I can tell you one thing," Daddy said, setting his pail down to admire the sky. "Only two days in a year like this one. The sun's sitting smack dab over the equator, so no matter where you are on earth you get just the same amount of night and day."

"That so?" Chig asked.

"You might be a sailor on the South China Sea, an Eskimo up in an igloo, or a nomad out on your camel in the

Sahara desert. Don't matter. We all get an equal gift of night and day from the old Creator."

Chig hadn't understood it all at first. "How does it work?" she'd asked, and her daddy had gotten the globe and a kerosene lamp down from the mantelpiece. The lamp was the sun, and Chig had held it so Culpepper County (marked with a pushpin on the globe) got its full light. She'd learned to spell *vernal* (spring) and *equinox* (equal night). And she'd brought in the *Farmers' Almanac* from its usual spot in the outhouse to look for the date of the autumnal equinox that coming fall.

Even then, she hadn't thought of it as special knowledge. If her daddy brought it up over chores, surely other daddies did too. But Chig could see from the lack of hands in the classroom that other daddies hadn't been so thorough.

Tap, tap, tap! Miss Barkus was losing patience. She paused with her pointer resting on Chig's desktop. Was she accusing Chig of holding back? How could she know that Chig knew what nobody else did?

Chig started to raise a hand, but one glance toward the back row caught her short. There were all the snorters and chigger-bite itchers ready to have fun on her if she was wrong. Was she ready to take that kind of chance? Answering the question would be a kindness to Miss Barkus, who was working herself into a fine lather. It'd probably even convince Willy that the twenty-first wasn't Laurel's or Hardy's birthday. But no. Chig didn't dare speak. After all, it was one thing to show your knowledge at the supper table, tucked safe inside your family. Another to stand up in class before Ed Beemis and all creation.

So no one found out what she knew. They never heard about Aunt Verna, who lived in Ohio now and sadly seldom visited. They never knew about the sunset she and her daddy had shared, so large and deep and lovely.

Chig thought for sure Miss Barkus would call on her to spill the beans. But her teacher looked through her, as if she weren't even there. Grabbing her globe, Miss Barkus launched into what looked to be a long explanation.

Chig reached a hand up her dress sleeve and pinched herself ever so slightly. She felt the pain, so she knew she must still be there. She hadn't become invisible yet, but maybe she'd come close. Only Willy seemed to notice her discomfort, the way her breath came in gasps and her cheeks flushed red. He arched an eyebrow her way.

Just this once, Chig ignored him. From the hurt on his face, she could tell she wasn't invisible to Willy. Not yet.

In the schoolyard at recess, Willy gave Chig some distance. She marched alone along the edges of the other scholars' play, kicking at the dirt. She gave the earth mean, solid kicks, the kind she wished her braver, better self might give her own shins. That was what she needed, she figured, if she was ever going to speak up and keep from going invisible. Chig was so absorbed in the feel of unyielding dirt against her boot toe that she nearly crashed into Ed Beemis.

"Hold on there, Miss Chigger," Ed said. "You're going to knock over a flea if you don't watch out."

The big boys behind him laughed, but Chig was in no mood for jokes. She glared at Ed, not caring for a moment what kind of reaction her look might bring.

"It's early in the season," said Ed, testing the dirt of the schoolyard with his shoe, "but I think the ground's solid enough for a tolerable game of ringer. Wouldn't you agree?"

Chig couldn't disagree. The ground was so hard she'd stubbed both toes kicking at it. "Yep," she mumbled, fearing where the conversation was headed.

"Seems to me you and that Huddleston boy challenged me to a game some time back," he went on. "I'm ready. Are you?"

How could Ed have known how unready Chig felt? How her marbles pulled at her jacket pocket like lead cannonballs? How her shooting arm hung low and heavy at her side? Not even her mouth seemed to be working right. She was struggling to get words out when Willy came to her side.

"Oh, she's ready," he told Ed. "But she'd like to grab a

copy of *Chilter's* from the library corner before getting started."

"That so?" Ed asked.

"Yep," said Chig, her voice finally working again. She turned tail and raced into the schoolhouse. Back in the library corner was a worn copy of *Chilter's*, purchased by Miss Barkus on her summer book-buying trip to a secondhand store in Indianapolis. Chig pulled it off the shelf. She considered for a moment grabbing the Bible, too, but a loud, gonglike noise jerked her back. The sound scared her nearly as much as Chandu the Magician's gong always scared Hubie. She shook herself, wished for some of Chandu's magical powers, and headed out the door.

One of the big boys was banging a stick on the trash can lid, announcing the start of the game.

"Here's *Chilter's*," Chig said, thrusting the book into Willy's hands.

No one needed to consult the book on how to get started. Both players would toss from the taw line to determine who would play first. Ed crouched down and gave a good throw. His shooter stopped about as close to the opposite lag line as it could come without rolling past. Next, Chig stood, knees quaking, and tossed her marble onto the ground.

She caught a glimpse of a frown on Willy's face. Her

shooter rolled an inch or two short of Ed's. If only she'd had a growth spurt. Then her shooting arm might have had the strength and power it needed now.

Ed started attacking the marbles arranged in an X on the ground. He shot three of Chig's nicest ones out of the circle and scooped them up.

"Good playing," one of the big boys called.

In the silence, someone let out a sigh of disgust.

"What're you doing taking Chig's marbles?" Alberta asked. "You've got a drawerful of them at home you don't even play with. Why do you need more?"

"It's a sport, Alberta," Ed answered. "You wouldn't understand." Then he paused to wipe his hands on his red bandana.

Something stopped his rhythm. Ed's next shot was way short. Chig hunkered down and studied the ring. It was still full of marbles. Full of possibilities even for a girl whose shooting arm could use a little more power and strength.

Chuck-ah! Ker-chuck! Without a word, she set to work. She captured first one, then two of Ed's marbles. Soon she'd grabbed more of his than he'd taken of hers.

"Thatta girl!" Willy said. "Go to it!"

And she would have, if a faint yelling toward Niplak's center hadn't grown louder and more urgent.

"Ed! Alberta!" a voice called. Soon old Floyd Wild

from the broom factory could be seen trudging up the hill.

"There's been an accident," he said breathlessly when he reached the schoolyard. "At the Saw and Haul. Your dad's hurt. Your mom needs help. Get down there quick."

Ed didn't stop to gather his marbles. He didn't stop to say good-bye to Chig or anyone else. He raced ahead of Alberta down the path to town.

10

A SHOULDER TO TAP

Mr. Beemis survived a close shave with his own saw. After the doctors got through with him, he was laid up for a good long while. Alberta returned to school two weeks later, her eyes downcast. But as soon as recess came, she was talking excitedly about the blood and gore and how those Indianapolis doctors had managed to put her daddy back together again with just a hundred and ten stitches.

Chig saw Ed only from a distance that spring. From the lectern at the Church of Our Redeemer, he asked for the congregation's prayers of healing. Chig didn't see him again at school. At thirteen, he was through with education. Ed was running the Saw and Haul, with help from Buzz Hawthorne, Mr. Beemis's right-hand man.

Chig couldn't say exactly why, but from time to time, she caught herself almost missing Ed. Maybe it was because, for good or bad, he never let anyone feel invisible. Now when Willy gave a silly answer (as he usually did) to one of Miss Barkus's questions, the usual chortles from the back row were absent. When Chig failed to reach the top shelf of the bookcase, she turned around, half fearing, half wishing to hear Ed's whispered "Pah-*teet!*"

She had no reason to fear. Not only was Ed safely out of the picture, but somewhere late that spring or early that summer, Chig grew a quarter inch. She was a full four feet two inches, not far shy of Granny Shorty in stocking feet. It wasn't exactly a spurt (Hubie shot up two inches in the same brief time), but it wasn't shrinking, either. It was maybe even proof that modern nutrition could produce excellent results in juveniles, especially a juvenile like Chig who always cleaned her plate. But Chig doubted that you could hold off invisibility by quarter inches. She needed more dramatic results—and soon.

That summer, just as they had the summer before, Chig and Willy met up from time to time at the schoolyard to play marbles. On his birthday, Willy's grandfolks on his mama's side had come through with a rainbow of marbles to refill his deerskin pouch. He no longer had to borrow from Chig to play, and it gave him a boldness he'd previously lacked. Now he played to win.

Hot sun and soft muggy air pressed down, turning the hilltops around the Niplak school a hazy blue-green. Willy's slow and easy ways perfectly matched the days until Chig pulled out her pouch and asked, "Wanna play?" Then Willy's eyes shone like the sky blue immie he'd once swapped to Georgie Gibson for a taste of chocolate.

Chig had always done well under Willy's coaching, but she did even better when playing for keeps. She learned so much from losing her own marbles—and from taking one or two of his—that she decided to ask Willy for advice on a more serious matter. After all, a boy who could teach her to hold her own at marbles might know a thing or two about the rest of life.

"Hey, Willy," said Chig.

"Huh?" he asked.

"Ever know anybody as small as me?"

Willy stopped arranging the marbles for their next game to give Chig's question his full attention. It was as if he needed time to order his thoughts with care.

"Can't say as I have," he answered, "but then again, I've never been out of county. Your granny Shorty's just a slip of a lady. But even . . ."

Willy's voice trailed off.

"But even she's got some height on me," Chig finished for him.

"Yep. And more flesh, too," Willy said. (Granny Shorty Kalpin was a bit on the fleshy side.)

"Supposing a small person wanted to be bigger," Chig said, "how would they do it?"

"I seen you eat," Willy said slowly. "That ain't the problem."

"Nope."

Willy picked up two marbles and clicked them in his palm to help himself think.

"Hey," he said after a click or two. "I got an idea."

"Oh, yeah?"

"Sure," he went on. "It's like Miss Barkus always says: 'If you're unsure, turn a page or tap a shoulder.'"

Chig hadn't heard this one of her teacher's sayings. It didn't quite have the zing of "You can lead a horse to water . . ." In fact, it didn't make much sense at all to Chig.

When he saw Chig's confusion, Willy explained. "See, Chig, if you need to find an answer, you can look it up in a book or ask someone who knows more'n you do."

"I already looked it up in a book," said Chig. "All it got me was a quarter inch."

"Anyhow," Willy said, "the book wagon's not due back till school starts. But isn't an expert in bigness coming to town a week from today?"

An expert in bigness? Coming to Niplak? And Willy even knew what day? Chig dropped her marbles in awe. Then she let out a gasp.

"The tall lady!" she said. "That's what you're on about."

"Am I right?"

For a boy who'd never advanced from the small seats at Miss Barkus's school, Willy Huddleston had a surprising number of hidden talents. Sure he was right. The very next Friday, Earl Dwight's Traveling Carnival was due to set up its tents in the center of town for the annual Niplak fair. And, as promised in the posters Chig had read and reread over the last few weeks, one of Mr. Dwight's star attractions was the world's tallest lady. Who would know better the secret to being big than that fine lady?

But how was Chig to learn the lady's secret?

Earlier that week, after Em had been put to bed for the night, Chig's daddy had made a troubling speech.

"Chig, Hubie," he said after clearing his throat several times. "I hate to disappoint you two, specially now that you're both tall enough to go on the big kid rides at the fair . . ."

Chig and Hubie exchanged looks. This was starting to sound like bad news.

". . . But," Daddy continued, "times are hard. Rides cost money. And cash money's the one thing we don't have."

"Can I still enter my squash?" Hubie asked hopefully.

"Surely, son," Daddy answered. "There's no charge for that. And I wouldn't be surprised if that squash of yours brought home a ribbon."

Hubie swelled with excitement and pride. He'd been watering and tending a squash plant for months now. He'd even fed it the water Mama usually dumped out after boiling potatoes. One of the plant's babies had grown bigger than the bed of the wheelbarrow. By the time of the Niplak fair, it threatened to be too big even for the back of the Model A.

When Daddy had given his speech, Chig hadn't been all that concerned. The Niplak fair was more than the three rides and half a dozen other attractions in Earl Dwight's Traveling Carnival. There was the produce show, where Hubie's squash looked to be a winner. There was the pie-baking contest, where Mama and Granny Shorty and most of Chig's aunts entered into friendly competition. And there was the spelling bee Miss Barkus put on each year, pitting her oldest scholars against Niplak's finest. With so much to see, Chig would hardly miss a few rides and attractions.

At least, that's what she'd thought then.

Willy's voice broke into her thoughts. "Now, if memory serves," he said, "it cost twenty cents to talk to the tall lady last year."

"Sure hope she hasn't raised her prices," Chig said.

"Darn tootin'," said Willy. Neither of them needed to tell the other that, with times as hard as they were, twenty cents was twenty cents more than they had. Mama's hens weren't laying, so Chig wouldn't be getting her usual share of the egg money. How was she to earn one penny, let alone twenty?

"Well," said Willy, "we don't both have to go."

"What do you mean?" Chig asked.

"All we have to do is get enough money together for one of us to visit the tall lady," Willy answered. "And that one of us should be you."

Here was Willy Huddleston offering to give his own money so that Chig could see the tall lady! Of course, he didn't have any money. But the offer itself was downright generous. If he hadn't just captured three of Chig's marbles—and shown no remorse whatsoever—she'd have called him a gentleman to his face. Instead, she pumped him for more advice.

"But how are we going to earn twenty cents in one week?" she asked.

"Your guess is as good as mine."

Able-bodied men were having trouble finding work. Niplak was usually too out of the way for trends to take notice of it, but this was different. The whole country, including Culpepper County, was in the middle of a Great

Depression. How on earth were a scrawny, lazy boy and an undersized girl going to find jobs when grown men couldn't?

This was one nut they weren't going to crack in a day.

"Meet you at the big rock on Monday," Chig said. "That'll give us both time to think."

"I'm thinking already," said Willy. It looked as if the effort was causing him pain, but he agreed to meet Chig on Niplak's main street after the weekend. Maybe by then, Chig hoped, they'd have an idea between the two of them. If not, perhaps Niplak, in all its grandeur, would inspire them.

11

TIGHT SPACES AND A SHOOK RICK

In downtown Niplak, just beyond reach of the sorghum mill's old mule, was the big rock. It had been left behind by a glacier that had visited the county some ten thousand years before. No one had thought to move it when Niplak was founded. Instead, Main Street jogged around it, giving anyone who cared to clamber up the rock's rounded sides a perfect view of all the town's goings-on.

Chig and Willy and countless other kids, past and present, loved the big rock. Large enough to prove a challenge for young mountain climbers in training, it was too small and hard to appeal to grown-ups. "Hey there," Chig whispered in greeting. She patted a warm, sunny side of the big rock's granite face and waited for Willy.

He wasn't long in coming. Even from fifty feet away, though, Chig could see that Willy had about as many bright ideas for making money as she did. Willy shuffled along as slowly as sorghum molasses pouring from a bottle on a winter day. He was bound to scuff the heels of his shoes to shreds if he kept it up, but Chig decided not to point this out to him. He looked as if he didn't need more bad news.

"Howdy, Chig," he said.

"Howdy."

"Can't for the life of me figure out how to make twenty cents, can you?"

"Nope."

They sat on the rock and squinted into the early-morning sun. The hilltops were lost in haze. A lone truck lumbered down the road but didn't pause in Niplak. Dew varnished the grass around the rock.

Although the day promised to be a scorcher, it was still cool enough to think. But even working their brains as hard as they could, Chig and Willy were short on thoughts. They'd begun to sweat a little from the effort and the midmorning heat when Jimmy and Timmy Settle, Daisy's older brothers, loped by.

The Settle twins were only recently graduated from

the Niplak school. Now they used their school smarts and big-rock-climbing skills in their very own painting business. "Never seen anything like those boys when it comes to climbing a ladder or putting up scaffolding," Chig's daddy had remarked not long before. Chig and her daddy had been standing in front of the Gibson place on East Main, where the Settle boys were deep into painting gingerbread trim on the eaves.

Jimmy had chatted with them during a root beer break. "Mrs. Gibson's sister Tallulah is coming down from Chicago for a visit next week," he'd explained, "so we're painting the whole place up, inside and out."

Now he greeted Chig and Willy with a halfhearted wave. "Good day for rock sitting," he said.

"Yep," Chig answered.

"Sure beats painting," Timmy said, setting his buckets and brushes down on the grass.

Willy and Chig perked up. Didn't Timmy and Jimmy seem a bit cranky and tired?

"If you're too wore out," Willy said, "we'd be happy to do your job for a day."

"And we'd only charge twenty cents for the both of us," Chig added quickly.

"Now, hold on there," Timmy said. "I'm not so beat yet that I'd hire two whippersnappers like you to fill in for me."

"Nope," Jimmy added. "Anyhow, it's not tiredness that's got us down."

"What is it?" Chig asked. She'd never seen those two without heaps and heaps of energy. Something had surely gone wrong.

"It's the tight spaces," Jimmy explained.

Timmy nodded in forlorn agreement. "Yep," he said, "Mrs. Gibson is a stickler for getting plenty of paint into all the tight spaces—inside cupboards, under the eaves . . ."

"Even back behind the bathtub!" Jimmy added. "A person would have to work mighty hard just to find out there's a wall there, let alone paint it."

"And Mrs. Gibson works that hard?" Chig guessed.

"You got it," Timmy said. "Gets down on her hands and knees, she does, and holds a mirror out under that tub just to show you where you missed."

"That so?" Willy asked.

Jimmy and Timmy's long looks said it better than words could.

"I'm good on the straightaways," said Jimmy, "and Timmy's a whiz on window and door trim. But those tight spaces . . . why, you'd have to be tiny just to get your arm in to paint 'em."

Chig and Willy looked at each other, their smiles spreading. "What about me?" Chig asked. "I could get into tight spaces for you."

"Ever done any painting?" Timmy was already looking less long in the face.

"Helped my daddy whitewash the henhouse this spring," Chig said.

"Think you could you paint all Mrs. Gibson's tight spaces for ten cents?" Jimmy asked.

"Sure could," Chig answered, "but I'd rather do it for twenty."

Jimmy scratched his head and frowned. "Can't make it that rich, Chig, and still cover my costs. But if you're interested, the original offer still stands."

"Ten cents would be most generous," Chig answered. Getting a paying job of any kind was such a stroke of luck, she didn't want to sound greedy. And ten cents meant that only ten cents more stood between her and a meeting with the tall lady.

"You wouldn't happen to have a job for me, would you?" Willy asked.

"Sorry," Timmy answered, gathering up his buckets and brushes. "You may be scrawny, but you're still too big for the tight spaces crew."

The boys were already heading off for the Gibson place, so Chig only had time for a quick word of encouragement. "You never know when good luck will strike again," she said.

"True enough," Willy said. He looked ready to keep

his place on the big rock until more good luck unseated him.

Chig found him planted there the next day. She climbed up next to him, dug a hand into a pocket, and pulled out two shiny nickels. Paint still stuck under her fingernails and speckled her hair.

"Was it hard work?" Willy asked.

"Nope," Chig answered.

"What was it like back behind the Gibsons' bathtub?" Willy asked. Like the Kaplins, his family did their weekly bathing in a tin tub set in front of the kitchen stove. A permanent indoor tub, in a room all its own, was something to think about.

"Tight," Chig answered.

They were still considering the Gibsons' tub when a two-horse team clomped up to the big rock. The team's driver, Buzz Hawthorne, looped the reins around a nearby hitching post and adjusted his rig. As a longtime employee of Beemis's Saw and Haul, Buzz was used to pulling all kinds of things. He and his team had dragged tractors out of ditches and pulled dozens of stubborn stumps from the ground. Now they were hauling a long flatbed wagon ready to be piled high with logs for sawing. With Mr. Beemis still laid up and Ed manning the office, Buzz was on his own.

"Fine morning for tree cuttin'," Willy called out.

"Yep," Buzz answered. "But by the time I get this rig out to the Evans place, it's bound to be hotter than Hades."

"You working for Miss Evans?" Willy asked.

"Yep."

Chig was relieved that Buzz was as big and burly as he was. He wouldn't have anything to fear from Editha Evans's stick.

"It's going to be a long day, being shorthanded like we are at the Saw and Haul," Buzz went on.

Willy was already on his feet, ready to leap from the big rock and make up any kind of shorthandedness Buzz might be suffering from.

"Yep," said Buzz, eying Willy with new interest. "I could use a hand gathering firewood. You good with kindling, boy?"

"I can shake a rick in no time flat," Willy answered. Chig gazed at her friend in amazement. She'd never seen him hurry to do anything other than eat. And here he was offering to stack firewood, fill the empty spots in the rick with kindling, and do it all fast.

Buzz looked skeptical. Huddlestons weren't known for their get-up-and-go. "I could only pay you five cents for an afternoon's work," he said. "And you'd have to keep out of old Editha's way. She don't care much for children."

"True enough," Chig said.

But neither the prospect of a swat from Editha nor the

promise of mere pennies for hard work discouraged Willy. "Deal," he said, leaping down from the rock.

Such a run of good luck was bound to end badly. Willy was so tuckered out from working and from keeping himself out of Editha's reach that he slept late on Thursday. Chig had nearly given up hope of seeing him when he finally dragged himself into town that afternoon. He slumped onto a low granite roll of the big rock. Then he reached deep into a pocket, pulled out his marble bag, and tipped out immies and aggies and five copper pennies.

"You hold on to them, Chig," he said.

"No, I couldn't."

"Sure you could," Willy said. "Anyhow, I'm betting your pockets are less apt to leak than mine."

Chig looked Willy up and down and took the pennies. Even before he'd gone into the woods at Editha Evans's place and helped Buzz haul and stack tree limbs and kindling, his pants had been in sorry shape. They were not improved by their encounters with brambles and thorns and twigs.

"How long you figure we got?" Willy asked.

" 'Spect they'll start setting up the tents tonight," Chig answered. "The fair starts at nine. That gives us eighteen hours, long as we don't sleep."

"I can't promise I can stay up all night working, Chig," said Willy.

No, Chig allowed. Willy didn't look as if he'd be awake for more than ten minutes. Between the two of them they'd managed to earn fifteen cents. But there was no sign of more paying work on the horizon. And they were running out of time and energy.

What agony to have come so far and still be a nickel short.

"Maybe it's best we sleep on it and meet back here first thing tomorrow," Chig said.

Willy raised a droopy eyebrow. "There you're talking," he mumbled before dozing off in the afternoon sun.

12

THE WORLD'S TALLEST LADY

Friday dawned warm and damp. The skies seemed to want to rain but lacked the will to do it. Instead, muggy wetness hung in the air, pressing in on the tents and wagons of Earl Dwight's Traveling Carnival. From their vantage point on the big rock, Chig and Willy watched for signs of life. They had set their sights on a tired-looking green tent that slouched next to a sign proclaiming WORLD'S TALLEST LADY—SEE HER STAND! ASK HER QUESTIONS! EXAMINE HER WARDROBE! ONLY 20 CENTS!

Squash judging was set to begin at nine A.M. sharp, so Chig's time was limited. So were her ideas for raising that last nickel. Could she ask her folks? Not likely. Not after they'd already told her they were short on cash money. Could Willy ask his folks for a loan? Surely not. The Huddlestons had never had much to spare, even before hard times had hit the county.

"Got any notions?" Willy asked as squash judging drew near.

"Nope."

"Well," said Willy, easing down from the big rock, "there's still time."

Chig didn't answer.

"Leastways," Willy said, "if things are hopeless, we might as well try to distract ourselves. Let's go see about Hubie's squash."

Already Willy had to raise his voice a bit to be heard over the sounds of cars sputtering, chickens squawking, and cheery voices calling—all signs of the start of the Niplak fair. Those sounds had reached a gentle roar by the time the two had a chance to sit together again on the big rock. It was late afternoon, after Hubie's squash had won a red ribbon, after picnic lunches, and after Aunt Ida's pecan pie had taken top honors. The spelling bee wasn't set to start for an hour. Chig and Willy took advantage of the lull to think.

From time to time, they watched as citizens of Niplak bought a ticket from Earl Dwight, pulled up the flap of the tall lady's tent, and disappeared into the darkness. When they emerged ten minutes later, they looked dazed—

perhaps by the light of day, perhaps by the revelations of the tall lady. It was hard to tell.

"There's got to be a way in there," said Willy.

He was sounding desperate, as if he hoped to find a chigger-sized tear in the tent. Chig was, she figured, just about small enough to slip into that tent unnoticed, but she couldn't cheat Mr. Dwight. If only . . .

"Hey!" said Chig, springing up from the rock. "It just might work."

Chig didn't give Willy a chance to ask for details. But he too sprang from the rock, following her as she zipped along to the ticket booth.

"Afternoon, Mr. Dwight," she said, standing almost tall enough to be seen.

"What?" Earl Dwight asked. From the look on his face, it was clear he thought the air itself was talking, but then Chig hopped up into view.

"I got a proposition," she said.

"That so?"

"Yep."

"What is it?" asked Mr. Dwight. Ticket buyers were growing scarce as the afternoon waned. Mr. Dwight wasn't averse to spending a little time talking.

"I reckon I'm not as big as most of your customers," she said. "So why not let me talk to the tall lady for half price?"

Earl Dwight chewed on the stub end of a pencil and jiggled the change in his pocket. "Half price is too low," he said, "even for a half-pint like you."

"How about twelve cents?" Chig countered.

"Still not enough."

"Fifteen?"

"You drive a hard bargain, young lady," Mr. Dwight said, handing Chig a paper ticket. He jiggled Chig's change into his pocket and pointed the way to the tall lady's tent.

Chig's feet barely touched the grassy ground. She half heard Willy call out, "Give her shoulder a good tapping, Chig!" before she lifted the flap and plunged into the darkness.

It was so dim inside that Chig stumbled. She was expecting a more exotic interior—like the settings Chandu the Magician found himself in—with Persian rugs, statues of Egyptian gods, and perhaps a thronelike chair. But as she struggled to her feet, all she saw was a pair of knobby knees. She hadn't meant to start out on such poor footing, but here she was looking up the dress of the tallest lady in the world! It was a vast dress, yards and yards of cotton clumsily stitched together, most likely by the long, bony hands that dangled at Chig's eye level.

Chig looked up to a long, pale face. The tall lady had a head full of frizzy red-brown hair, much like Chig's own.

She wore gold hoop earrings that dangled down toward stooped shoulders. Chig couldn't figure why a tall lady wouldn't stand tall. But maybe with all her excess height she didn't need to.

"You must be near eight feet," said Chig, forgetting her manners and her usual "Howdy-do."

"More like seven," the tall lady said. She didn't seem put off by Chig's lack of manners. She answered the question with a matter-of-factness that reminded Chig of her daddy or Miss Barkus.

Most grown-ups and tall folks took a while figuring out where Chig's small voice was coming from. But the tall lady saw and heard Chig right away. She stared down with piercing green eyes, daring Chig to say more.

Chig could feel words rushing around in her head, but for the moment she was too stunned to talk. No doubt about it, seven feet was tall. Chig stood on tiptoe but still had trouble taking her all in. Then she saw again one of the tall lady's slumped shoulders. A shoulder to tap.

Chatterboxes and busybodies had never been high on Chig's list. She hated to seem like one herself. But if she stayed quiet, she couldn't learn much from the expert in bigness looming before her. If she stayed quiet, she'd waste five of Willy Huddleston's hard-earned pennies, as well as two of her own nickels. And though she knew Willy would try not to show it, he'd be sure to ache with disappointment if Chig chose this moment to be as silent as a chigger.

"What's the secret to being big?" Chig asked. There it was. She'd gone and blurted out the question she'd been holding in for so long. Never before had she had so much hope that she might find an answer.

"The secret?" the tall lady asked. "It's no secret, far as I can tell."

"Then how'd you get to be so big and tall?"

"Well," the tall lady answered, "I was born big, got bigger every year, and didn't stop growing until last January."

"What stopped you then?" Chig asked.

"It was a mighty cold January," she said, "but I don't think that's what stopped me growing. I figure I was done. That's all."

The tall lady made it sound so simple. But there had to be more to it, didn't there? Chig wanted to think there was, but finally, in the quiet darkness of the tall lady's tent, she gave in to despair.

"Oh," she wailed, "I'd give anything to be as big and tall as you are!"

"My land, girl," the tall lady said. Her voice turned soft and soothing. "You should thank your lucky stars you're not my size."

Chig looked up, startled.

"Sure," the tall lady went on, "it may seem glamorous to be the tall lady and have your own tent." She waved a bony hand at the cramped army-green surroundings. "But you should count your blessings that you're not so big you bonk your head on nine out of ten doorways. That you don't have to buy the whole bolt of cloth when you want to make a new dress. That you don't need to put a chair at the end of your bed at night just so's your feet will have a place to rest, too."

The tall lady looked exhausted by her speech, or maybe it was just her feet that were worn out.

"Are they tired?" Chig asked, pointing down at shoes that looked to be a size thirteen or bigger.

"I'd say my arches have just about fallen down," the tall lady answered. "Course, I have to stand when I've got paying customers. Sitting down, I don't look so big."

"You can sit down for me," said Chig. "I don't mind."

"I'm much obliged," said the tall lady, easing her bulk into a folding chair. She leaned over and massaged the arches of her feet.

"Ever been invisible?" Chig asked.

The tall lady eyed Chig and considered. "Nope," she said, "but wouldn't that be a hoot. To go into a room and not have everyone staring at you."

Chig was about to say she'd gotten her fifteen cents'

worth when the tall lady gave her a tap on the shoulder. "Anything else you'd like to know?"

Anything else? Well, sure . . .

"If you could be any size," Chig began, "any size you wanted, what would you be?"

"Hmm." The tall lady leaned back in the folding chair, hiked up her dress, and flexed her toes. What would be full-length black stockings on anyone else came up only an inch beyond her knees. "Any size?"

"Yep, any size at all," said Chig.

"Well, then, I'd still be tall," she answered. "Not tallest-lady-in-the-world tall, but pretty big all the same. You get used to a certain view, you know, and it's hard to imagine seeing the world any other way."

"That so?" asked Chig.

"Yep."

Chig thanked the lady for her time and left her in the gloom to wait for her next customer. The tallest lady in the world was still massaging her sore feet when Chig looked back one last time.

13

TOWN, TRAINS, AND TALK ABOUT THE WEATHER

So there was no big secret after all. It was a lot of food for thought, what the world's tallest lady had said. A heaping plateful. Chig worked her way through it slowly, like the careful eater and thinker she was. It made her quieter than usual—as silent as a chigger bent on getting in a few more bites during the last warm evenings of summer and fall.

Chig was so busy thinking that she didn't notice when the next quarter of an inch crept up on her. But there it was on the closet door, four feet two and one-quarter inches from the floor:

Chig M. Kalpin, age 10, Sept. 9, 1935 ————

Sure, it was progress. But at this rate it'd be 1957 before she hit five feet. Hubie was only six, but he was already taller than his little big sister. Even Em, now a lanky toddler, was inching up on Chig.

It was enough to make Chig sigh. And these weren't the usual sighs of a quiet girl. They were long and low and sad. Sad as the call of the mourning dove that sat on a soggy tree branch just outside the Kalpins' kitchen window.

When Mama suggested one Saturday early that fall that Chig take a walk into town, Chig nearly flew out the screen door. Hubie was hauling firewood with Daddy. Em was too small to go along, and Chig knew Willy wouldn't be able to join her either. It was too damp and chilly for marbles or for perching on the big rock. And Willy was needed at home, where his mama was expecting a new baby. But even without anyone to talk to or sit with, Niplak had its charms.

"Only a quarter mile left to Niplak," she said to herself, crossing the bridge.

Chig thought she could see her daddy's fine handiwork in the half-rusted railings and the pockmarked cement bridge deck. She always stopped to toss boats of curled sycamore bark off one side, racing to the other to watch them bob downstream. As she breathed in the damp of the creek, Chig's eyelids fluttered closed. She could almost see how hard it must nave been in her great-great-granddaddy's day to ford the creek. Anytime but deep summer, when the creek dried to a trickle, you'd have been up to your kneecaps or hubcaps in water.

A rhythmic shaking of the railing left red rust dots in the warm creases of Chig's palms. Her eyes flew open. Almost immediately she spied the source of the shaking: the 10:40 A.M. train. She waved to the engineer and scanned the boxcars for signs of hoboes. Had anyone riding on the 10:40 had breakfast with the Reverend Granddaddy Lukens that morning? But no. Chig saw no sign of men riding the rails. Instead, the engineer answered her wave as the train rolled closer to the railroad trestle bridge.

Engineers for the Indiana Hilltopper Railroad Company had chosen the widest and most steeply banked stretch of creek to cross when they'd set down tracks in the summer of 1901. Not two hundred feet from the county bridge was a creaking, hill-high heap of wooden beams and steel rails. The best thing about the railroad bridge was its length. Even at the widest point in the creek, a bridge didn't have far to go. This one was so short that once the engineer sped over it, he could be reasonably sure that all the other cars would make it too. Or he'd know the bad news before the minute was up.

The old bridge threatened and protested and gave out moans of complaint every time a train crossed. Sometimes

Chig even heard its moans when it was trainless and suffering under a stiff breeze. But it had never made good yet on its threats.

Chig knew the railroad very nearly hadn't come to the county. It was, Miss Barkus had explained, all due to an error on the part of one of the engineers. "That is why, scholars," she concluded, "I am sometimes tolerant of mathematical errors in out-of-county folks. I do, of course, hold you to a higher standard." Chig did her best to measure up.

As it was, the tracks nicked the county's northern corner, passing right through town. Not that the train usually stopped. Mr. Gibson from the dry goods store held a bag of outgoing U.S. mail on the end of a long stick. If all went well, a man in the mail car first tossed a bag of incoming somewhere in the vicinity of Niplak. Then he grabbed Mr. Gibson's offering. It was a dance of great precision. Not too different, Chig guessed, from what ballet must be like, although perhaps less graceful. She had gone to Niplak many a time just for the joy of watching Mr. Gibson's dance. So had most of her classmates and even most of the grown-ups in town, back when they'd been young and in their shine.

Chig hurried to find out what news, if any, had dropped in with the 10:40. She hoisted herself up the stone steps into H. J. Gibson's Dry Goods. Once she was inside, the gloom of the high, overstocked shelves shut out all light. Chig waited for a moment or two until her eyes could make out the stacks of galvanized pails, pairs of stiff blue overalls, and row upon row of canned goods. Near the register, where Mr. Gibson had already retaken his post, was a display of penny candies.

A few pennies were in fact at that instant burning and itching and sweating in Chig's palm. They were her share of Mama's egg money. Every morning, Chig watered and fed the hens while her mother did the more delicate work of stealing their eggs. Every evening, Chig checked that Margaret Dumont, Queen Victoria, and all the birds were snug on their roosts and all the windows and doors of the henhouse carefully locked against foxes, raccoons, and coyotes. After a dry spell in the heat of summer, the hens had started laying again. So once every week, if Mama had spare eggs to sell to the man who drove the grocery wagon, she chose the shiniest pennies in her purse for Chig.

"There you are, Chig," Mama would say. "You sure earned it."

"Yep," Chig would answer. "I reckon I did."

With cash money as tight as it was, Chig had more than once been asked to donate her pennies right back to the family's grocery fund—a pile of change in an old Mason jar. But this time, Mama hadn't asked. Instead, she'd urged Chig out the door with a "Scoot along, girlie."

Now at the dry goods store, Chig selected a few candies. Some were for her and some for Hubie. Em was content with the empty wrappers. Miss Barkus's constant drilling in math allowed Chig to figure out in her head all the possible combinations of gumdrops, horehound sticks, and cinnamon balls. For this Chig was immensely grateful. She pushed her candies and her cash onto the counter. Then she waited to be seen. Having recently had a close-up view of the underside of Mr. Gibson's bathtub, Chig was, for the moment, too shy to talk. Instead, she coughed.

Mr. Gibson set down his paper and peered over the counter. Chig hopped, her head appearing just at the high counter's edge.

"That you, Chig?"

"Yep."

"That be all for you today?" he asked.

"I reckon."

Mr. Gibson tucked the candies into a brown paper envelope. Chig coughed again—a cough that sounded like a question.

"Didn't see you at the mail drop, Chig," Mr. Gibson ventured.

"Nope," Chig answered.

"Reckon you'd like to know how it went."

"I'd be obliged."

"Well, it was a perfect drop, Chig, if I do say so my-self," said Mr. Gibson, his eyes twinkling. "The outgoing went off smooth as silk, and for once the incoming missed the puddles."

"Now, there's a comfort," Chig said. Mr. Gibson gave her the candies and a warm smile.

Clearly, to Mr. Gibson, she hadn't become invisible yet. Maybe it was like her daddy said, though, that people were bound to make a fuss over you if you had money in your pocket. But Mr. Gibson's smile gave her hope that he might have noticed her even without her shiny pennies. It gave her courage. She figured she'd try her luck next by Mr. Gibson's stove.

In one corner of the store was a huge potbellied stove, which in winter glowed red with a high-banked fire. Around it were arranged several grown-up men who had something better to do but who hadn't gotten around to doing it quite yet. In the meantime, testing Gibson's chairs with their weight was a reasonable substitute. Some days, the men got so deep into conversation Chig doubted they'd notice a hurricane. But she hoped that if she stood tall enough, they might notice her. Or if they didn't, she hoped they'd be talking about something worth sharing with her family over the noon meal.

Uncle Elwin was there, sorting the mail on his lap be-fore starting out on his postal route. Willy Huddleston's daddy was there, lazily chewing a wad of tobacco. They were part of a handful of regulars, joined this morning by someone whose backside Chig didn't recognize.

She inched closer. The stove wasn't lit this early in the season, and she dawdled behind its bulk. Then she saw it: a crisp red bandana poking out of the new fellow's pants pocket. It was just Chig's bad luck that Ed Beemis was taking a break from the Saw and Haul.

Usually Chig counted on the chair testers to fill her in on the latest news from Niplak and the world beyond. Sometimes the men pondered great issues of the day, debating points raised in the president's latest radio chat. At times, they simply gossiped. Once or twice they discussed who was hiring for what and for how long. For the most part, however, they studied the weather. It was one of Chig's favorite topics. Normally she would edge over to Uncle Elwin's elbow and ask him for his two-day forecast. This time, however, she faded into the shadows cast by the stove, hoping against hope that no one would see her.

"Had a right smart of wind over at our place last night," said one man who'd traveled in from a distant holler.

The other men were silent for a moment, not sure what to make of this renegade fall wind. Finally, the talk shifted to long-range forecasting.

"I was talking to Jack Forbst the other day," Uncle Elwin began.

"Oh, yeah?" the others said. Several set their chair legs down gently and leaned closer. Sure, Elwin knew his way around a rain cloud, but Jack Forbst was a known authority on the weather.

"Well, the way he tells it," Elwin went on, "hornets' nests are thicker this fall than he's ever seen, and caterpillar coats are full and downright glossy. Looks like a wet fall, snowy winter, and wet spring to come, says old Jack."

"That so?"

Chig longed to know more. She very nearly spoke up and asked Uncle Elwin what Mr. Forbst had said about woodchucks—the thickness of their coats was generally a good predictor of winter weather. But suddenly the new fellow leaned back his chair, caught sight of the small figure hiding behind the stove, and—ever so softly—snorted.

"Catching a cold, Ed?" one man asked.

"Could be," Ed said darkly.

Chig very nearly slipped out of Gibson's without saying another word. But a nagging thought bothered her. Even though she'd seen Ed from afar at the Church of Our Redeemer, she'd never gotten up the courage to talk to him since that day when they'd both hunkered down in the schoolyard. She had something of his that needed returning.

"Ed," she said.

He looked up, his eyes rimmed red. Perhaps he was getting a cold after all. Chig felt confused but went on. "I got some marbles of yours from that game we never finished. Want me to bring 'em to church tomorrow?"

"Nope! Got no need for 'em now."

"But don't you want to play marbles with me again?" Chig asked.

"That's a child's game!" he said, putting his chair legs down with a crash. "I've given up such things."

Was Ed really finished with marbles and other games? Chig couldn't tell from the way he said it if he meant it or if he was just afraid he'd lose. Surrounded by all the grown men at Gibson's, he suddenly looked older. But could you become a grown-up in an instant? Would you want to?

Chig didn't wait to find out. She shot out from under the shadow of the stove and through the door. She didn't stop running until she saw her family's cabin, tucked safely on the crest of a small hill.

When she got inside and set down her brown bag, the rest of the family was already at the dinner table. After the usual blessing and "Please pass the salts", Chig delivered the local version of the twelve o'clock news, careful to leave out Ed Beemis's cold. "Well," she began, "the incoming didn't puddle, and Mr. Gibson had a good send-off." Chig's high red color could easily be mistaken for a flush worked up hurrying to make it home for dinner. She caught her breath and went on: the sorghum mule was still making his rounds. The broom factory was closed, but it was closed anyhow on weekends and any number of weekdays, too. And according to Jack Forbst, the long-range forecast was for wet all the way through spring.

"That should make for a bumper crop of chiggers come summer," said Daddy with a wink.

"I 'spect so," Chig answered, piling Mama's fresh cottage cheese on her plate. Cottage cheese, besides being truly tasty, was, according to Aunt Dorothea, full of protein and calcium. And there was an off chance that protein and calcium might help even a little slip of a girl like Chig grow bigger and braver and more visible by something more than a quarter inch at a time.

14

SECOND SPREAD

"**B**aby Pearl's already twelve pounds and twenty-three inches," Willy said one October day. "Papa says if he'd known she was going to be such a chunk, he wouldn'ta given her such a small name."

Willy gave regular reports on his new baby sister to anyone who would listen. As other classmates grew tired of the updates, only Chig was left. Much as Chig liked Willy, Pearl was starting to get to her.

When the latest report had Pearl at twenty-four inches—nearly half Chig's height—Chig lost patience. "If she keeps it up," she blurted out, "that baby's going to eat you all out of house and home."

Willy gulped hard. He drummed his fingers on the desktop, then opened up his reader. Chig had never seen him show an interest in his schoolbook before. Was it something she said? Was Pearl that big an eater? Or, more to the point, were the Huddlestons spreading meals so thin that a hungry Pearl could eat them out of their home?

Willy paged through his reader all the way to the index, then started back at the beginning again. That was answer enough for Chig. She steered the conversation onto safer ground. "Sure is soggy out," she said, scraping mud off a boot toe with one end of her ruler.

"Yep," Willy said.

"Course, I've seen worse," Chig said, hoping to draw Willy out. But Willy didn't answer. Indeed, the fall of 1935 was wetter than normal. In years past, this fact would have left Chig with a sinking feeling of dismay. In years past, Chig had all too often been sucked in by the mud.

Chig had learned not to play in the schoolyard on the muddiest days. She could always sit at her desk and read during recess. But she couldn't avoid the mud on her way to and from school. The main road to Niplak and the Niplak school was generally quite firm, except during thaws. And the shortcut Chig took from her back door through the brambles to the side road held few surprises. But the short stretch of side road leading from the path's end to the county road was a soft, muddy sponge. Warm springs fed into it at several points, so it firmed up only in the heat of summer or during winter's coldest blasts.

Off and on, the county road crew talked about finding a solution, maybe even moving the road. But now that the crew was working reduced hours, and most of those in summer, such talk had stopped. Once each spring when the road quivered like jelly, the crew dumped a load of new stone on top. Within hours, the hungry earth sucked each piece of gravel down deep below the surface.

"When I was your age," Daddy had told Chig, "back about 1909, one of the road crew's older trucks got sucked down in the side road and was never seen again. Didn't even get a chance to set down its load."

Chig had given Daddy a wary look.

"No, it's true," he had gone on. "The driver jumped clear before the truck disappeared and lived to tell the tale."

Chig was never sure how much of her daddy's stories to believe, but she walked the road carefully, respectfully. Some days she stayed on the center crown, where bits of gravel hung on for dear life. Other days she walked the grassy verge. But always she tried to avoid the mushy tread lines in between. Her legs being shorter than normal, she couldn't always clear the mush. More than once, she'd found herself stuck fast in the middle of the road.

"Got sucked in again?" Hubie would ask. When Chig

had first started going to school, Hubie would often check to see if she made it to the main road. If he couldn't pull her out with a hand from the verge, he'd troop back home to find Mama. Mrs. Kalpin was city raised but strong as an ox. She made short work of pulling Chig out, scraping most of the mud off her boots, and setting her on her way while Hubie cheered.

Only once had things gone from bad to worse. That day, in her struggles to free herself from the road's muddy grasp, Chig had lost her lunch bag in the muck. Hubie had found her crying. "What a terrible waste of good food," Chig had said between sobs, "and my favorite sandwich, too!" Mama fixed a new lunch as good as the first. But well over a year later, Chig still viewed that particular spot of road with an injured suspicion.

In the fall of 1935, more than one spot in the road threatened to suck down an unsuspecting lunch bag or small child. But that fall, Hubie was finally old enough to go to school. A good head taller than Chig, he was strong enough and good-natured enough to pull his little big sister out of almost any fix.

"I won't be late to school no more, Miss Barkus," Chig had said on the first day of school, beaming at her brother.

"*Anymore*," said Miss Barkus, but she too seemed happy to have Hubie in their midst.

Normally, a scholar as bright as Chig would have

moved up a row or two or more in the years she'd been at-
tending school. Each year brought new, fresh faces like
Hubie's, shining with the morning's cleaning and ready to
learn. But no year as yet had brought a new scholar
smaller than Chig Kalpin. "I must ask, in the interests of
efficiency," Miss Barkus said, "that you stay in the smallest
seat just one year more, Chig."

Chig understood. Hubie and any of the other new
scholars would find it a chore to press themselves into or
squeeze out of Chig's tiny desk. Willy Huddleston, still as
lazy as ever, had enough trouble getting in and out of the
small desk next to hers. Hubie was assigned the seat on
Willy's other side.

At lunchtime, the morning's light drizzle turned to a
downpour. Hopes for munching sandwiches while
perched on the near-horizontal limb of the old sycamore
were put by. Chig and the others pulled their prizes from
small buckets or pails or paper sacks. Drops of water from
the leak near the chimney hissed and pinged off the top of
the stove, still hot from its morning firing. The mood grew
warm and expansive.

"Is that any good or is it grunt?" asked Hubie, pointing at Willy's buttermilk biscuit sandwich. Chig told herself she'd have to give Hubie a talking-to about not being
quite so nosy. Then she eyed Willy's sandwich with interest. It was a simple affair: one biscuit, likely leftover from

supper the night before, cut in half and spread with ketchup.

"It's not grunt," Willy said in a tone meant to justify something. "The ketchup's homemade."

Chig saw at once what the problem was. Her own sandwich had come to school carefully tucked into an envelope of waxed paper. Willy's had come straight out of the bag, and it wasn't clear that any more biscuits lay waiting inside. A single sandwich was more than sufficient to feed a growing Chig, but you didn't have to be a dietitian to see that a boy like Willy needed stronger stuff. What was more, his sandwich had only one thing spread between its covers. Chig's had a layer of leftover mashed potatoes topped with a neat row of cold, cooked string beans. Opened up, the sandwich looked like a fancy colored postcard view of a green picket fence against a field of old snow. Hubie had insisted on his favorite: a quarter-inch slice of onion, topped with generous amounts of salt and pepper, sitting on a thin layer of peanut butter. All this between slices of their mama's homemade bread.

For as long as anyone could remember, hardly a soul in the county had ever had money to speak of. But while cash had never flowed in the county, Chig understood that most folks had reserves. A sandwich with only a single spread pointed to a disturbing lack of reserves.

At Chig's house, even when the road crew cut Daddy's

hours again and again, there were always the three milk cows, the laying hens, and the few acres of bottomland that supported a good garden and one field each of sorghum and corn. Mama had her egg money. Plus, she made such fine cottage cheese that people often drove or rode up of a Saturday, hoping to buy a jar. These were her family's reserves against hunger. Chig had never questioned them before. She'd never imagined a sandwich with just one spread between its covers. Yet she saw hunger in Willy's eyes, hunger for a second spread.

Both she and Willy were eating slowly, Chig out of habit, Willy out of self-restraint. "My mama says your mama makes darn good ketchup," Chig told Willy. "You mind swapping half sandwiches?"

Willy had his pocketknife out in an instant, slicing each sandwich in half and licking the crumbs from the blade.

Chig hoped the good Lord would forgive her for using such strong language. She was so unused to lying that the *darn* had slipped out unbidden. She knew God would forgive her the lie. Even if Mrs. Kalpin had never spoken of Willy's mama's ketchup, it was awfully, awfully tasty. Almost tasty enough to make Chig forget the lack of a second spread.

15

SEARCHING FOR SPREADS

"**H**ubie," Chig said on the way home from school. "You can't be such a busybody and ask folks what's in their sandwiches."

"Why not? You wanted to know too."

He had a point. Now that Willy's sandwich was revealed to be lacking a second spread, Chig was curious to peer into the lunch pails of all the other scholars at the Niplak school. How many others were suffering from a lack of reserves?

Chig only had to listen to the talk at the dinner table on Sundays or the chatter around the potbellied stove at Gibson's to know that the depression was getting worse.

Or maybe, as Daddy put it, the depression was the same as ever, but folks were losing patience with it as it dragged on and on.

At school the next day, Chig sidled up to Alberta Beemis at the coatrack and snuck a peek into her small galvanized pail.

"Hey," she said, trying to see what lay under the tidy red-checkered napkin on top. The Beemises, Chig could tell, were doing fine, at least for now. With all the biscuits tucked into that pail, Alberta sure wasn't going hungry. But hadn't Chig seen her friend eating biscuits more often than not in the last few months? Hadn't Chig herself eaten them more often than in years past?

"Hey," Alberta answered.

"Ed sure did a nice job on the scripture reading last Sunday," Chig said. She meant to steer the conversation away from lunch pails—to hide her interest—and Ed was about as far away as she could steer. He was mean as a hornet off church grounds, but even Chig had to admit that he was a model of good Christian behavior during Sunday services. What a puzzle.

"Alberta," Chig went on, "I tried to give Ed back some marbles the other day, and he said he'd never play again—not me, not nobody. You got any notion why?"

"Things change," Alberta explained while the two girls moved toward their seats. She looked around, as if making sure she wouldn't be overheard. "He's been ornery ever since Dad told him he couldn't be a preacher two years back."

"A preacher?"

"Sure," said Alberta. "He was all hepped up on it—loves standing in front of a crowd—but Dad says there's no money in it. Sawing and hauling are sure things, he says, and that's what Ed's got to do. What with the depression and all, beggars can't be choosers."

"Nope," Chig agreed.

"Not that we're beggars," Alberta backtracked. "But anyhow, when Dad got laid up, Ed had to do what he didn't want sooner than he'd been dreading."

Alberta paused to put her books inside her desk. "He's ornerier than ever, I tell you. Sometimes I think he's saying if he can't be a preacher, he might as well be a devil."

Dring! Miss Barkus's bell marked the beginning of lessons. Chig raced to her seat and thought about what Alberta had said. On radio shows like *Chandu the Magician*, the evildoer was always a plain vanilla kind of evil. "One hundred and ten percent evil," as Hubie said. Chig and Hubie always rooted for Chandu to get the villain, and, using his magical powers, he always did. It was satisfying that way. But it had never occurred to Chig that an evildoer like Roxor might have his reasons for being bad. That maybe he was doing evil just to spite someone who'd said he couldn't do good. Life and Ed Beemis were more of a puzzle than ever.

As fall turned to winter and Chig managed to peek into lunch pails and brown paper bags, she came to see that the biggest puzzle of all was finding something more to spread between the covers of sandwiches. Most of the lunches she'd spied were decidedly slim on spreads.

When a midwinter thaw turned the schoolyard dirt to a jellylike mass, Chig chose to stay indoors at recess. Of course, Hubie could have pulled her out of the muck if she'd gotten sucked in. But this day, she wanted Miss Barkus's advice. This was one puzzle she couldn't figure out all on her own.

At recess, Miss Barkus allowed herself the privilege of pulling her chair over by the woodstove and basking in the warmth. Two of her oldest, most trusted scholars served as playground monitors—watching for fistfights and missed turns at hopscotch—so Teacher could have a break each day. Today, a week-old copy of the Chicago Tribune rustled in Miss Barkus's hands.

"You're not going out, Chig?" she asked, glancing over the paper toward the door. "Can't count on much more warmish weather like this until spring."

"Yep," said Chig. "That's what Jack Forbst says, too. Says it'll be a snowy winter, for the most part, and a wetter-than-normal spring."

"That so?"

"Yep."

A log inside the stove popped and crackled.

"What's on your mind, Chig?" Miss Barkus asked at last.

"Spreads. That's what."

"Spreads?"

It took a while for Chig to explain what she meant. How lunch pails at the Niplak school were lighter than she could remember in her two and a half years as a scholar. Along the way, she talked about the crowd of men at Gibson's and how it was larger each time she went to Niplak. And how her parents had been asking her, once again, to put her share of the egg money into the family's cash jar.

"I see," said Miss Barkus. "What do you plan to do?"

"Me? But I thought you'd have the answers."

Miss Barkus put her newspaper aside with a decisive rustling. "I've read all about this depression we're having, and the alphabet soup of fixes the president is hoping will put us back on course. And I sure don't know what'll make things better."

"But I'm talking about something to spread on sandwiches," Chig said. "Not about the depression."

"Aren't you?" Miss Barkus focused her most penetrating gaze on Chig. "Seems to me if people around Niplak had more work, they'd be bringing home more money. Then lunch pails would be fuller, and there might even be some change to spare for penny candies at Gibson's."

"I'm not in this for the candy!" Chig protested.

"Course not," said Miss Barkus. "You're in this because you care. I have faith in you, Chig M. Kalpin. If you set your mind to this business of spreads, I think you'll find a way."

Chig wasn't nearly so confident. She was almost glad when the first scholars rushed back to warm themselves by the stove before the bell brought everyone in for lessons. They made such a clatter Chig almost didn't hear her teacher's last words on spreads:

"And when you've got an idea, I'm ready to help."

The thaw ended just after New Year's. A foot of snow fell with a wallop onto Niplak and the hills and hollers around town. The county road crew made no attempt to clear away the snow. There was no money in the budget for such luxuries. Another thaw was bound to come along soon. And after all, who was in that much of a hurry to get anywhere?

The few folks who had to get out on the roads did so gingerly and slowly. Chig's uncle Elwin, for example, stretched his usual postal route over several days, working even on Sundays to deliver the mail.

"As my old friend Herodotus used to say, neither snow, nor rain, nor heat, nor gloom of night stays this courier from the swift completion of his appointed rounds." With that, Uncle Elwin plopped down into the Kalpins' easy chair for a rest late one Sunday afternoon. Mama served him a plate of dinner leftovers, kept warm by the stove, and soon he no longer looked gloomy at all.

"What's your forecast, Elwin?" Mama asked.

"Is it for thaw?" Chig added.

"Nope. No thaw in sight." He pointed his empty spoon at the snowy scene outside. "It's at times like these that a feller could use a little help. But of course, the U.S. Postal Service, in its great wisdom, doesn't believe that Niplak, Indiana, deserves its own post office."

Chig shook her head in sympathy.

"So here I slave away, all alone except for Gibson doing his part with the incoming and the outgoing."

Uncle Elwin looked so cozy and warm that Chig strained to imagine him working like a slave. Still, it couldn't be easy collecting stamp money from dark crannies in folks' mailboxes, putting on the stamps, and seeing that everything was properly sorted and delivered. Especially not all on his own. Chig nearly said so, to urge her uncle on. But Elwin didn't need any fuel for his fire.

"Did you hear what's going on in Hilltop?" he asked.

"Nope," said Chig. She was always interested to hear news from the county seat.

"Well, the U.S. Postal Service and the WPA have cooked up plans for a brand-new post office. They'll break ground for it come April."

"You mean the post office won't be in the basement of the courthouse anymore?" Mrs. Kalpin asked from the kitchen.

"Nope," said Elwin. "Since Hilltop's the county seat, they got the ears of the politicians."

He nodded at Chig. "That's how these things work. You got to have political pull, and that's one thing Niplak ain't got."

"But that's not how it's supposed to work, is it?" Chig asked. She knew from listening to the news that the WPA was a new addition to FDR's alphabet soup of agencies. It was a tallish short way of saying Works Progress Administration, and it was supposed to bring all kinds of building projects—and jobs—to folks who needed them. All the jobs were supposed to be divvied up fairly, but maybe it was hard for grown-ups to be as fair and decent as they could be.

"Don't think Niplak'll ever get its own P.O.," Elwin went on. "Not until someone important lives here."

Chig gazed out the window. Draped in billows of white, her corner of Niplak was downright beautiful. The best place on earth to live, hands down. She thought she could see smoke from the chimneys of all her friends and family smudging the sky. How could anyone want to live someplace else? But maybe truly important people needed more than beauty, family, and friends.

"Not a bad idea, Chig. Not bad a-tall." Miss Barkus was beaming down on her smallest scholar. She finished wiping the chalkboard and joined Chig by the fire for a recess rest.

"Could you help me figure out who to write to?" Chig asked. "A politician, maybe? Or someone at the WPA?"

When her teacher didn't answer, she went right on. "Just think of all the jobs there'd be building a P.O. And think of how much bigger everyone's sandwiches would get if there was a little cash to spare. If I ask those folks nice enough, they'll say yes to a new P.O., won't they?"

"Hate to burst your bubble," said Miss Barkus, "but it may not be as simple as all that."

"Oh?" Chig had the feeling that nothing was as simple as it might be.

"Even if you could find a politician or an official at the WPA to write to, they probably wouldn't take you seriously," Miss Barkus said.

"'Cause I'm so small?"

"No . . . yes." Chig's teacher stumbled with her answer. "It's because you're young. I doubt it would matter if you were the biggest almost-eleven-year-old on earth. Those politicians and officials are so busy with requests from grown-ups—folks with lots more clout than you have— they don't have a minute for letters from kids."

"What about FDR? Would he take me serious?"

"Seriously," Miss Barkus corrected her. "And I expect he would, Chig, but he's got bigger fish to fry. He's trying to make all the big plans to get the whole country out of the depression. He's got no time to make plans for a place as small as Niplak."

"Why don't you write the letter for me?" Chig asked. "The WPA or the White House is bound to take a lady as important as you seriously."

Miss Barkus smiled. Chig could even have sworn her teacher blushed. "No. This is your letter to write," she said finally. "But I'm thinking you could send your letter to a lady who's even more important than I am—and you just might get a reply."

It took a week of missed recesses and many false starts, but at last Chig was ready to put a stamp on the envelope. Miss Barkus helped her find the address. Then she wrote in her clearest scrawl:

Mrs. Franklin Delano Roosevelt
Office of the First Lady
The White House
1600 Pennsylvania Avenue
Washington, District of Columbia
U.S. of A.

16

THE GREAT FLOOD

Chig handed the envelope directly to Uncle Elwin to ensure its safe delivery. But she said nothing of its contents. Not to him, not to her parents, not even to Willy.

"Best not to get people's hopes up," Chig said to Miss Barkus.

"I expect you're right."

"Then if there's no answer, no one's disappointed," Chig explained.

"I could name two people who might be a bit downcast if it came to that," Miss Barkus said. "But I'm crossing my fingers for Eleanor Roosevelt to reply."

"You really think she might?"

"That was a fine letter you wrote, Chig," Miss Barkus said. "If Mrs. Roosevelt doesn't answer it, maybe she's not as decent as folks say she is."

Trying to be decent was hard, as Chig well knew. She hoped Mrs. FDR measured up to her tall name. In the meantime, she watched the mailbox and waited. And waited. All winter and into spring.

At school, Chig kept on swapping half sandwiches with Willy. She learned to savor the half with the second spread. She was happy to swap, but part of her worried. Was she getting enough modern nutrition? She hadn't had another quarter-inch—or smaller—spurt since fall.

Lately, she had been checking herself regularly against the closet door at home. She leaned back, heels pressed against the wood, spine stretched straight, one hand balancing a pencil level with the top of her head. She'd make a quick mark, then pivot to check her progress.

But no. The pencil marks refused to climb.

All she could hope for was a springtime spurt . . . and perhaps a little more food. Mama, Chig could tell, was stretching each jar of canned goods just a little farther than usual. Meat, except for salt pork, was becoming a rarity. More often than not, Sunday supper was not leftovers from dinner but cold corn bread broken up in a bowl of milk. Or fresh salted popcorn in milk for a special treat. Chig loved her mama's corn bread and positively craved wet popcorn, so she had no complaints. But she felt a creeping uncertainty.

By the middle of March, the days were warming feebly as the winds shifted and came out of the South. For twenty days straight or more there had been a little or a lot of rain in and around Niplak. The men drying out by the stove at Gibson's compared the recent weather to floods of the Bible. They even nicknamed young Georgie Gibson Noah, seeing how he was restoring a worn-out old canoe and planning to paddle it all the way to the Ohio River. "Take me with you, Noah!" the men would call out whenever poor Georgie chanced to be at the store.

Chig didn't see the humor in the situation. Her daddy's bottomland was flooded, and only a good long spell of dry weather would make it firm enough for spring planting. The road crew had lost one of its trucks while fording a too-deep creek, and the county was struggling to find the money to replace it. Shorter hours for the road crew seemed likely.

One especially soggy Saturday, Chig made a startling discovery while watering and feeding the hens.

"Queen Victoria is dead!" she said, the screen door flapping behind her. She was dripping a puddle of rainwater on the kitchen rug, but Mama didn't seem to notice. Maybe, Chig guessed, she was wondering how many fewer eggs Queen Victoria's death would mean to the Kalpin table. Victoria could always be counted on to lay a queen's ransom of eggs, even when times were at their bleakest.

"Well," Mama said finally, "you got to look for the silver lining in the dark cloud."

Chig gave a questioning look.

"And that means baked chicken for dinner," Mama said.

Baked chicken! How long had it been since they'd had any? And wasn't it about the tastiest food in the world? Even a tough old laying hen like Queen Victoria was likely to turn tender under Chig's mama's care. Chig's mouth was already watering.

"My lands," Mama said. "I'm fresh out of sage and thyme." She pulled the Mason jar down from the cupboard and fished out a quarter. If they were to be feasting on the queen at noon, someone needed to make a run to the dry goods store for spices.

"I'll go," said Chig. She could hardly get any wetter than she was. And a trip to town would give her a chance to view the creek's high water up close. It was already so high she could hear its roaring at night when the house was still.

Hubie was pressed into a too-small raincoat. He would be going along strictly as a safety measure. He wasn't good enough yet at figuring to be trusted on his own with grocery money. But what with the state of the roads, Chig could not be trusted to survive a walk to town alone.

Chig clutched Mama's quarter and called back through the screen door, "We're off to Niplak!"

Mama had asked them to hurry, but the two couldn't help dawdling for a while at the metal bridge. Chig remembered now hearing cracks of thunder in the night and the pounding of a heavy downpour that had broken her dreams. Below the bridge she and Hubie could see the aftereffects of that storm. Torrents of water raged by. Chig's sycamore-bark boats bobbed and twirled for a second at most before being pulled down into oblivion by the current.

The base of the bridge—Mr. Kalpin's handiwork for sure—held strong and firm, even as sticks and small logs lodged against it. The same could not be said for the railroad bridge. Never before had Chig heard such moaning and sighing from the wooden trestles. Naturally quiet herself, she was more than a little embarrassed by the bridge's complaints. Before averting her eyes, however, she saw something that made her heart jump.

"Lord have mercy," she said softly.

The rushing water was slamming a log again and again against the wooden bridge. Chig's ears adjusted to the constant roar of the water so she could hear the log's regular pounding just above the din. Already one of the timbers looked to be giving way.

"What time is it, Hubie?" Chig asked.

"On about nine of the A.M.," he answered.

"You see what I see?" Chig pointed to the railroad bridge as it gave out an especially loud moan.

"Yep."

"Daddy would know what to do, wouldn't he?" Chig said.

"Sure," answered Hubie, "but he's clearing brush for that new field up from the creek. No way he can get here and fix the bridge in time. Not all by himself."

"Nope," said Chig. "And the ten-forty is an awful punctual train." The only chance Chig saw lay in the crowd sure to be testing the chairs around Mr. Gibson's stove. She took a deep breath and yelled, "Race you to Gibson's!"

Hubie speeded ahead. Chig ran as quickly as she could, taking care not to land in the spongiest road sections. But that effort grabbed only half her thoughts. Her mind raced. How could they repair the bridge in time?

Each of the men at Gibson's, Chig knew, had something to offer: Uncle Elwin had a generally dependable truck. Buzz Hawthorne and his team of horses had the strength of ten men. And Mr. Huddleston was a world-class gatherer of odds and ends; he'd be sure to have something you could use to patch together a quick fix for a sagging bridge. Others might help too, if only there was time. But who could lead them? Chig hoped against hope that one of the chair testers would rise to the occasion.

Hubie got to town first. At least, that was what Chig figured must have happened. Nearing Niplak, she heard a gonglike sound. She guessed it might be the clatter of Hubie scattering a stack of metal pails across Mr. Gibson's wood floors. And anything that close to the sound of the gong on *Chandu the Magician* was bound to make Hubie too scared to talk.

Chig pushed her legs to move faster. Her eyes watered from the run. Her breath came in wet gasps. Magical powers sure would have helped, but you couldn't count on them if you weren't someone like Chandu.

Chig burst into Gibson's and said the first thing that came to mind. "We got a chicken to cook, and the railroad bridge is just about to go!"

"Hold on there now. What did you say?" Mr. Gibson set his newspaper on the counter and peered down at Chig's dripping, frizzy head.

"There's not much time, I reckon," Chig said, turning toward the crowd by the stove. "A big old log was ramming the timbers when me and Hubie went by a few minutes ago."

"Hubie and I," said a female voice from the corner where the work shirts were stacked.

Chig let out a soggy sigh of relief. If anyone could get the men organized, Miss Barkus could. People who'd grown up in the county were used to following her orders with meek obedience.

"Saints preserve us!" Mr. Gibson said. "What on earth can we do? That train's already long since gone through Martinsville. No way to stop it now."

He looked down at Chig, who was holding on to her brother's hand. "You and Hubie best run along home and keep safe."

Chig would have none of it. "Hubert," she said firmly, "take Mama's quarter and tell her and Daddy what's going on. I'll be down at the bridge helping Miss Barkus."

"You sure, Chig?"

If Chig noticed the slight wail in Hubie's voice, she never let on. "Sure, I'm sure," she said. "Now run along home like Mr. Gibson said."

Chig raced to Uncle Elwin's side. He and the other chair testers were already trying out ideas on Miss Barkus.

"We could make a net out of ropes and sling it underneath to catch anyone or anything that falls when the bridge goes," suggested Buzz Hawthorne.

"We could build a rock wall across the tracks in the

field before the bridge," said Ed Beemis. "That'd stop a train."

"We could—"

"Quiet!" Everyone was silent, barely daring to breathe. "Buzz," said Miss Barkus, "your idea shows great originality. And yours, Ed, would be fine if we had the time. But we need quick, small, practical fixes." She paused. "I'm not sure just what will work, but I have faith in all of you. When you've got an idea, I'm ready to help."

The chair testers stayed silent and forlorn. Miss Barkus's encouragements weren't having their usual effect on them. But Chig glowed in the warmth of her teacher's familiar words. She hopped on one foot, then the other. When that didn't get Miss Barkus's attention, Chig coughed.

"Yes, Chig?" Miss Barkus asked.

"I was just thinking," Chig said. "Couldn't some of these fellas do a quick fix on that old bridge?"

"I quite agree with your thinking. But we need answers, plans, ideas—"

"Maybe I got some ideas," Chig said softly.

Miss Barkus gazed down on her smallest scholar. A few of the men around the stove set their chairs flat and leaned forward. Ed Beemis snorted, but he listened too.

"Well," Chig began, "first thing is to get on down to the bridge." Everyone nodded. Chig turned to Buzz

Hawthorne. "Your towrope and horse team might come in handy."

Buzz shot up from his chair, said "Yep," and headed out the door.

"Uncle Elwin," Chig went on, "could you drive on down to the Settle place and pick up Jimmy and Timmy? I'm thinking we could use some good climbers."

"No trouble at all," said Uncle Elwin, grabbing his coat.

"Mr. Huddleston," Chig asked, "you got some hammers and nails you could bring?"

"Sure thing," he answered as he strode out of the store. "I'll rustle up a few at home."

Chig turned to Ed Beemis, took a deep breath, and plunged on. "Ed," she asked, "could you hurry down in your dad's truck with any spare boards you've got at the Saw and Haul?" Chig figured no one would stop Ed for underage driving during a crisis. He, like most boys in Niplak, had done years of practice driving on the family tractor and would be itching for a chance to take the wheel. But the chance to drive was not enough to sway Ed.

"You're not going to let that little chigger order us around, are you?" he asked, whirling to face the other chair testers.

"Got a better idea?" one asked.

Storm clouds seemed to be gathering around Ed, but before the thunder boomed, Chig said, "Ed did have a great idea. It just needs a few adjustments." She paused and tried to smile at Ed. "We may not have time to build a wall, but we can still do some warning. Now, someone go with Ed and gather up as many red bandanas as you can at his house."

Ed sputtered but couldn't get a word out before Chig went on.

"You fellas meet in the field on the far side of the bridge. Grab yourselves some sticks and make warning flags with Ed's bandanas. There's half a chance you can stop that train before it gets to the bridge."

"My hankies! I'm not giving up my hankies!" Ed cried.

"It'd be a loan, Ed," Chig explained. "And they'll make as good a barrier as a rock wall on short notice."

Ed snorted once or twice, but he raced out the door.

In a matter of minutes, a raggedy caravan of trucks and wagons and children on foot headed out of Niplak for the railroad bridge. Chig and Miss Barkus piled into the back of a horse-drawn wagon trotting along at a good clip. Bouncing in the back, Chig wondered how she'd managed to get so many words and ideas out at once. She was so lost in thought she almost didn't hear Miss Barkus say, "Wasn't I right in having faith in you all?"

Hubie made better time than Chig thought possible. He and Daddy and Buzz Hawthorne were already in conference by the trestle bridge with the Settle twins and Uncle Elwin when she arrived. Brakes squealed when Ed pulled up in Mr. Beemis's truck, the back piled high with planks.

From the road crew's sturdy metal bridge, Miss Barkus observed the scene much as a general surveys his troops. She kept an eye on her pocket watch. Chig's teacher took pride in having an accurate timepiece and in knowing how time was measured. On this day, time was running dangerously short.

Chig joined Willy when he and Mr. Huddleston arrived bearing hammers and bags of long, strong nails.

"What're they going to do?" Willy asked.

"Buzz'll lower the twins partway down on towropes so they can shore up the bridge with some planks," Chig explained, drawing closer to the muddy banks.

"Think it'll work?" Willy asked.

"It's worth a try," Chig said.

Above the roar of the water, Chig soon heard both the pounding of logs thrust against the timbers by the flood and the pounding of nails repairing the damage. Even though it was still raining slightly, Chig thought she could see sweat breaking out on Jimmy Settle's back. Timmy too hammered away as if there were no tomorrow, until Miss Barkus shouted, "It's ten-thirty!" Fear must have opened up her windpipes—Chig's teacher's bark was louder than usual. The crowd of onlookers drew back. Hubie pressed up against Chig's side, trembling.

"It's going to be all right, Hubie," Chig said. Then she wondered, was it?

"Are we ready?" Buzz Hawthorne shouted.

Jimmy and Timmy Settle, raised up once more from the churning waters, nodded. "Ready as we'll ever be."

In that moment's silence, Chig saw Ed Beemis leave the safety of the crowd and walk toward the tracks.

"Ed?" Buzz Hawthorne said.

But Ed only gestured as if to say "It's okay" and continued. He stopped just short of the tracks, then raised a hand into the soggy air. "Oh, Lord," he said, "may this bridge hold together and serve as a symbol of our willingness to join hands and do good work. . . ."

Chig's mouth dropped open. It was the first time she'd seen Ed act like a good Christian off church grounds. Maybe there was hope for him yet.

"We gather here . . ."

Whooping from across the field cut Ed's benediction short. He rejoined the safety of the crowd. In the distance, Chig could see a flurry of red flags waving as the chair testers did their job. It was hard to say if they had the intended effect. The train's engineer, unused to any kind of communication with Niplakians, sped by.

Miss Barkus's careful teaching to the contrary, Chig could have sworn that time stood still. Certainly, no one spoke. The air was heavy with the engine's roar, the rush of water, the timbers' moans. Through it all, Chig heard the song of a chickadee, apparently unconcerned by all that was going on around it.

Today's Hilltopper wasn't very long. Chig silently counted the cars as they raced by. First the engine shot past, then the tender, next the baggage car, the mail car, then the three passenger cars, and one, two, three, four, five freight cars. Pigs were in one of the last cars to make it over, but their squeals were drowned out.

Bridge timbers screamed, popped, and hissed. Hubie clung to Chig, and Chig clung right back. Even as it was happening, Chig caught herself thinking this was something she would never, ever forget. She'd see it again in her mind—and maybe in her nightmares. She'd feel this fear again if she sniffed a whiff of steam from an engine or felt the earth rumble this way under her small feet.

The bridge broke apart as cleanly and quickly as a dried-out wishbone from a chicken carcass. Cars twelve and thirteen swayed as tracks and trestles buckled and sank underneath. The earth shuddered in a way Chig knew only from scripture readings from the gloomiest bits of the Bible. The downward pull was so fierce that the last freight car sheared off from the rest of the train before it could cross over. It nose-dived into the water, digging deep into the creek bed. If the current hadn't been raging so, Chig guessed, there might have been more of a splash as it hit the water.

Up above, the caboose somehow held firm on what was left of the trestle. It coasted forward, dragged by the motion of the rest of the train, still on its way to Niplak, and pulled to a stop by the last freight car, now half underwater. Soon the caboose too threatened to plunge into the swollen creek.

17

10:40 AND BEYOND

"**A**nybody in there?" Chig's daddy led the crowd of men who raced to the tracks, where the caboose held on for dear life. Every Hilltopper had an engineer and fireman in the engine and a conductor in the caboose. And anyone unhappy enough to be in the 10:40's caboose was in mortal danger.

"He's on his feet!" yelled Timmy Settle, who'd edged out onto the tracks to peer inside the caboose. Soon all eyes were following the progress of the conductor as he climbed out the rearmost window and crept gingerly down to grab Timmy's outstretched hand.

Chig and Willy and Hubie watched from the edge of

the crowd, near the creek's muddy banks. When both men landed on firm ground, a cheer went up.

"Shhh!" said Chig.

Willy gave her a puzzled look. Real-life heroes were rare in Niplak, and he was set on catching a glimpse of the Settle twins.

"I heard something," she explained. "Somewhere over there."

Chig turned toward the sound she thought she'd heard. "Over there" was in the raging creek. The water was a frothy yellow-brown. It looked a bit like chocolate pudding, but there was nothing sweet or smooth about it. It slapped brambles flat along the edges of the creek and slammed against the raised side of the freight car. Above the water, Chig spied two hands gripping the edge of the half-open, half-submerged freight car door. The water was rising fast. There was no time to waste.

"Looky there!" she yelled, pointing at the groping hands.

Willy whirled around. "Help me grab that towrope!" Chig said. A heavy coil lay not far from her feet. "And you, Hubie, tie the other end to the sycamore tree." Hubie was strong enough to haul the rope up a short stretch of creek bank on his own. Together, Chig and Willy struggled with the other end. How were they ever going to cast it across the water?

"Let me have at it!" Miss Barkus, from her perch on the road crew's bridge, had seen all. Now she plucked the rope from Chig's and Willy's arms, shouted a terse "Stand back!" and whipped the rope like a lasso over the water. It landed neatly by what appeared to be a very wet, very bedraggled man. At first, Chig saw only his top half as he grappled with the rope and the slippery doorway. Seconds passed, but they seemed like hours. Slowly the man eased the rest of his body into view. Miss Barkus motioned for him to hold tight to the rope and make his way across the creek. But the yellow-brown foam pulled him under almost at once.

"Is he still holding on?" Chig asked.

"Can't tell," Miss Barkus said. "But don't let go, no matter what."

Chig didn't let go, even when she felt she could pull no longer. Even when Miss Barkus and Willy slipped in the mud after one especially powerful heave-ho. While they scrambled back to their feet, Chig alone held the rope. Suddenly she saw a dark head bobbing close to shore. With a last hard tug, Chig and Willy and Miss Barkus landed the man like an overgrown catfish on the muddy shore.

"Sure am glad I read that book on rope throwing," Miss Barkus said.

"So am I, ma'am," said the man. Then he promptly lost consciousness.

As Chig picked herself up from the creek bank, she heard the train whistle. From the sound of it, she could tell that the engineer had no inkling of trouble.

"They've gone right through Niplak," Mr. Gibson said. "Bet they've puddled the incoming to boot." But even Mr. Gibson soon shrugged off such a minor concern. He and Chig and a whole crowd of Niplakians were gathering around the man from the freight car.

"Looks like a hobo," someone said, and Chig's eyes lit up. So hoboes did ride the 10:40 after all. He must have hopped on the train in Indianapolis, Chig decided, maybe after breakfast at the Reverend Granddaddy Luken's. And what a shock to his system it must have been to find himself up to his neck in cold water!

"Warmth," Miss Barkus said, looking this way and that. "He's in shock, and a patient in shock needs warmth more than anything. But where to find warmth out here . . ."

The soggy bank and swollen creek seemed unlikely to yield warmth before summer.

"I got a notion," Chig said, spotting her daddy's Model A. "I'll be right back with some warmth, Miss Barkus."

Running from truck cab to wagon seat, Chig borrowed a half-dozen old car blankets. Most were more moth hole than blanket, but they might warm up Miss Barkus's charge.

"Help me with his coat," said Miss Barkus. "It's soaking wet."

Chig and Willy grabbed the sleeves and tugged as hard as they could. Miss Barkus, with Hubie's help, wrapped the man in dry blankets and carried him up the bank. He was soon settled nicely in the vast rear seat of Doc Settle's Pierce-Arrow. Chig and Willy followed, dragging the sodden coat between them. When the man awoke, Doc Settle took his temperature and shone a light in his eyes while Miss Barkus assisted.

"I am Miss Barkus, Lily Barkus," Chig's teacher said, enunciating clearly. "You are just outside Niplak, Indiana."

"Pleased to meet you, I'm sure." The man's voice was weak, yet it matched Miss Barkus's politeness tone for tone. "I'm Ogden Newt."

"Howdy," Chig said, but Mr. Newt didn't answer. There was so much of Miss Barkus to take in that he could hardly be blamed for not noticing someone Chig's size.

She wanted to ask him all about his life as a hobo, but perhaps this wasn't the time or place. Instead, she began to fold Mr. Newt's coat into a neat pile. The coat resisted. Hard, rounded shapes weighed it down. Chig reached into a side pocket roomy enough to hold a change of clothes and pulled out a large tin can. Then another. The paper labels had been sucked off by the floodwaters. But the cans were otherwise undented and in good condition for their travels.

"These yours?" Chig tried to get Mr. Newt's attention, but a deafening groan drowned out her words. With a final moan, the caboose slid sideways, pushing the freight car farther downstream and plopping in next to it. By the time Chig and Willy reached the bank, both cars were being sucked under the surface. Chig rubbed her eyes once, then again. If she wasn't mistaken, the freight car was giving up shiny bubbles. Her old rubber ducky did much the same thing when held under in the tin tub on bath nights. But the freight car's bubbles were more substantial.

Chig considered the shiny, silvery bubbles. "Cans," she said finally. "Look at all them cans."

"Ain't it *those* cans, Chig?" Willy asked.

"I reckon you're right," Chig answered. "But what do you suppose is in them?" Without a word more, the two of them raced to a bend in the creek. A few cans were already caught among the branches and weeds near the bank. Chig fished one out with a stick and looked for the label, but the water had already unglued it.

"Got your knife handy, Willy?"

"You know it, Chig," Willy replied. He worked the lid off in no time flat and peered down at a pink, jellied mass within. "For the love of Pete. What do you figure?"

"Dunno," said Hubie, joining them by the water, "but I'm hungry. Mind if I try?" When Chig and Willy shook their heads, Hubie dug the end of a stick in and gave it a taste.

"Hmm. Deviled ham," he said. "Remember a year or so ago when Aunt Dorothea brought us some?"

Chig could indeed remember. "Deviled ham," she repeated, her mouth watering.

"Sounds like a handsome spread," Willy said hungrily.

Chig wanted so much to dig in, but she knew she had to keep her head clear. "You eat it. I got a thing or two to do."

She slipped on the muddy bank but plunged ahead toward the crowd. "First thing," she said to herself, "get folks to fish out those cans." She had an idea how.

Chig's voice at its loudest wouldn't carry far over the roar of the water. She didn't bother to yell. Instead, she worked at getting people's attention through persistence—the way a chigger might bite you into knowing it was there. "Hey there, Mr. Gibson? Mrs. Settle?" A few soft words and a sharp tug at a shirt or a dress sleeve usually brought some notice. And folks who'd already given Chig a car blanket were glad to hear of the promise of deviled ham in return. Being the Good Samaritan generally didn't bring instant rewards.

Niplakians young and old headed down to the creek to fish for cans.

"Second thing," Chig mumbled, "figure out what to do with them."

"What'd you say, Chig?" Willy asked. Deviled ham had given him the kind of energy he usually only mustered for playing marbles. He plopped three cans on the pile growing near Chig's feet.

"It's not like they really, truly belong to us," Chig said, looking down.

The sun was shining feebly from behind rain clouds. The wet cans glistened like silver pirate's treasure. Nearly all had lost their labels. How many held deviled ham? And what other wonders might be packed within?

"But if they're bobbing free and easy in our creek, they don't still belong to the Hilltopper Railroad, do they?" Willy asked. "Plus, finders is keepers, specially when the finder's got a good appetite."

He had a point. A train company that didn't even notice losing two cars and a trestle bridge could hardly need deviled ham as much as Niplakians did. God, Chig trusted, would understand. Chig's God had vast reserves, unlike some folks around Niplak.

Still, she felt a nagging sense that someone's permission was needed before all of Niplak dug in. She edged her way into the crowd around the Hilltopper's conductor. When she was close enough to be heard, she said, "Welcome to Niplak."

"Always wanted to drop in," he said, causing the crowd to roar.

"Sir," Chig continued, "if we was to find some cans from that there freight car"—she pointed into the creek—"could we fish 'em out and eat 'em?" She was thinking of Editha Evans and her hungry eyes. A can or two of near about anything would sure taste good after too many dinners of corn bread.

"Don't see why not," he answered. "The bigwigs at the Hilltopper might disagree, but I'm a firm believer in finders keepers."

18

THE GREAT NIPLAK TRAIN DISASTER

Chkkk, Chkkk! The sharp clicking noises came from under Buzz Hawthorne's beard. He told his horses just what to do. With a few soft words and a few well-aimed tugs, Chig had convinced Buzz to drive his team and wagon down the steep bank. A car or truck would have been mired up to its windows. But Buzz's team was used to worse than hauling cans through a spot of mud.

"Know where you want me to take them?" Buzz was piling cans on the wagon bed.

"Nope," Chig answered. "Not yet."

"Keep me posted."

"Sure thing," said Chig, only it wasn't. You couldn't

call it a sure thing when you'd only half figured out your problem. How was she going to spread the Hilltopper's bounty evenly over the hills and hollers of Niplak?

Chig looked around for inspiration. Miss Barkus might have an idea, but she was too busy reheating Mr. Newt. Chig's daddy might know, but he was knee deep in the creek, trying to free cans caught in the brambles at the water's edge.

There were only a few other idle onlookers gathered on the bank with Chig. One was Mr. Gibson. Chig had never seen him looking so downcast. "Awful shame," she said, "the incoming being puddled and all."

"What? Oh, Chig," he said, "that ain't the half of it."

"How do you mean?" she asked.

"With no ten-forty, there won't be any incoming to puddle. Heck. There won't be any outgoing neither."

Chig hadn't thought about how the 10:40's plunge would affect folks like Mr. Gibson. He'd lost his chance to dance each day and bring in the news of the world. Plus, Chig figured he couldn't be too pleased at the thought of Niplak's being flooded with free food, what with the shelves at the dry goods store already stocked with food you had to pay for. No wonder Mr. Gibson's whiskers were dripping. Chig guessed there were tears mixed in with the drizzle.

She might have left him alone in his misery. But how could she? Here was an expert on canned goods, a shoulder to tap if ever Chig had seen one. "Mr. Gibson," she asked, "how many cans you figure we got here?"

Mr. Gibson eyed the pile rising in the wagon bed. "I'd say you're looking at nine hundred or more."

"That many!"

"That many." He shot the words out like a squirrel spitting out bitter walnut hulls, hoping to find something better underneath.

"How many cans per family would that work out to?" Chig asked.

"Oh, on about nine per cabin, if you count all the folks in hollering distance of Niplak."

Hollering distance, Chig knew, was quite a ways. As far as you could pass news if you stood on the top of a hill and yelled it down into all the hollers and then the folks in the hollers yelled it up to the folks living on the farthest hilltops—and so on, until you got to the point where nobody cared about the news because they weren't friends or relations.

One hundred cabins in hollering distance was a lot of cabins. And nine cans per cabin might well put a dent in Mr. Gibson's business. But not for long.

"Hey, Mr. Gibson," Chig said, "I got a notion how you might get more folks to come to your store."

"You do?"

"Sure thing," said Chig. And this time, it felt sure.

"Where do the ones with labels go?" Willy asked.

"Down there," said Chig, reaching for more from the pile at her feet.

It was Monday morning. Normally, Willy and Chig would have been at school. But nothing was quite normal on the Monday after the Great Niplak Train Disaster. School was closed until the outhouse—a victim of the flood—could be rebuilt. (Chig had always thought it perched dangerously close to the creek. She was relieved to learn that its new site was far from the floodwaters.)

All that morning, Willy and Chig had been working to pull together the new Niplak Free Store. The heap of cans that Buzz Hawthorne had off-loaded over the weekend lay at their feet. Daddy and Hubie were searching the creek-banks for still more of the 10:40's cargo now that the floodwaters were receding. Chig and Willy stacked the rare cans that still had labels in a small wooden crate. It sat on the ground just below long rough shelves groaning with label-less mystery foods.

Mr. Gibson stuck his head out the back door of the dry goods store. "How's the work going?" he asked.

"Just fine," Chig answered. She hoped she sounded reassuring. Mr. Gibson was still a little skittish about having a free store behind his own store. Chig had gone over it again and again on the creek bank. How folks would come to town for the free stuff. And how they'd more than likely buy peppermint candies or a shovel or some Mason jar lids with all the money they didn't have to spend on whatever turned out to be in the cans. And how they'd be sure to shop at Gibson's in years to come on account of how nice Mr. Gibson had been after the flood and the train wreck.

Nope. Chig could tell from the wail in his voice that Mr. Gibson wasn't altogether sold on the idea. But she was pretty sure he'd come around.

Willy's dad had come around right off the bat. "What should it say?" he'd asked when Chig requested a sign.

"Whatever you like," Chig had answered. Still, she was a bit surprised by the message on the sign Mr. Huddleston donated to the Niplak Free Store.

Yep, it's Free
But don't take More than you Need
Beware the Curse on those who give in to Greed!

"What kind of curse is it?" asked Chig, imagining her fingernails falling out or her hair going straight if she yielded to temptation.

"Oh, it's nothing special," Willy answered. "Papa puts

curses on all his signs. Keeps folks from snatching them just for the wood.

"What about the muddy cans?" Willy asked after a long pause.

"I'll ask Mr. Gibson for a pail and some rags so we can clean them up good," Chig answered. Inside, she blinked to get her eyes used to the gloom. Two or three of the chair testers put their chair legs down when they saw her come in. They nodded and smiled her way. Chig blinked again from surprise.

"Hey, Chig," another chair tester called out.

"Hey, Uncle Elwin," she answered. "What's the forecast?"

"Don't have the heart to think about the weather," he said. "Generally speaking, a man can count on taxes, the weather, and the mail." He sighed, then went on. "The weather's just about done us in, and unless I drive all the way up to the main station in Indianapolis, I'm not sure where the mail's coming from. I heard tell they lost a whole truckload of mail in high water. That leaves taxes."

"Not much comfort in taxes," Chig said.

"Nope."

When men stopped caring to talk about the weather, things sure were bad. It was hard for Chig to imagine them getting much worse, but just then a newish-looking sedan pulled up in front of the store. A fellow wearing a suit with lapels wider than Grandpa Kalpin's thighs walked through the door.

"Gibson?" he said, striding down the narrow aisle and nearly walking through Chig. He didn't wait for Mr. Gibson to answer but stuck out a hand for a quick shake. "B. T. Thorough, here, from the Indiana Hilltopper Railroad Company."

Chig shouldn't have been surprised. Someone from the railroad was bound to turn up sometime to check on the bridge, caboose, and freight car, even after Doc Settle had driven the conductor back to Indianapolis safe and sound. But she wished she hadn't been standing front and center, holding a slightly dented and muddy piece of the Hilltopper's cargo, when they did. Sure, the Hilltopper didn't need the cans as much as folks around Niplak did. But technically, the Hilltopper still owned them. And it was only polite to ask if Mr. B. T. Thorough wanted them back.

"Mr. Thorough," she said. But he was too busy talking.

"Gibson," he said, in a too-familiar city way, "we at the Hilltopper are quite impressed by you people, quite impressed."

"Mr. Thorough," Chig said again.

"Why, the way you people took care of our conductor is admirable. I understand from a Dr. Settle that the man came through the ordeal without a scratch.

"And without your quick action," he went on, waving vaguely at the chair testers by the stove, "I thoroughly believe that things would have been worse, much worse. As it is, we mean to rebuild as quick as we can. Get things back on track, if you get my drift."

"Mr. Thorough?"

"What? Yes?" he asked. He looked this way and that, finally settling on Chig's frizzy-topped head.

"We got some of your cans," Chig said.

"Cans?" he said. "My cans?"

"The Hilltopper's," Chig answered. "From the freight car that got sucked into the creek." She held up a mud-caked can to help Mr. Thorough understand. "You want them back?"

"Little girl," said Mr. Thorough, leaning down toward Chig, "if you can salvage a can or two out of this great disaster, you're more than welcome."

"Really? Truly? I mean, it's more than a can or two," Chig protested. But Mr. Thorough was already leaning away and beaming a benevolent smile at the chair testers.

Uncle Elwin turned a smirk into a cough. Buzz Hawthorne set his chair legs down with a smack and spat squarely into the spittoon by the stove. No one quite had the heart to try to set Thorough straight.

Chig whispered a request to Mr. Gibson for a pail and two rags. He brought out his largest tarp too, just in case Mr. Thorough should happen to stride by.

"No reason why he's got to know exactly how many cans you helped yourself to," Mr. Gibson explained.

"'Spect not," Chig said.

When it was time to stop for lunch, Chig and Willy leaned back to admire their work. Only a few hundred cans were still to be cleaned and sorted. Chig's fingers were chapped and her muscles ached. Cans didn't weigh much on their own, but once you got into the hundreds, they gave a body a good working.

"I'm tuckered," said Willy, chomping on a half sandwich.

"So am I," said Chig. "And this isn't even the hard part."

"How do you figure?" asked Willy.

"Well," said Chig, "we got to get the word out. Get our store some customers. And the only way I can see of doing that is to call on all the cabins around Niplak."

"You mean we got to walk to 'em?"

"Yep."

Willy's groaning was cut short when the back door opened. "Quick!" He grabbed one end of the tarp and Chig the other.

"It's only me," said Uncle Elwin. "Thorough's already on his way to Indianapolis. Suppose I should be getting on my way with the mail." Letters and newspapers from the last incoming drop were stuffed into Uncle Elwin's blue canvas bag. It usually sat beside him on the front seat of his Studebaker truck. Most days, Elwin held his shoulders high when he carried the mail. Today, Chig's uncle drooped.

"Hey, Uncle Elwin," Chig said. "If you haven't got much mail to deliver, would you be willing to deliver the news? You know, let folks on your rural route know about the free store and the cans?"

Elwin raised one eyebrow out of its droop when Chig explained her plan. Before long, he raised the other one too. "It'll take a few days—maybe a week—to let everyone know," he said, scratching his chin. "I'll have to cover my route in stages. Folks do like to talk once you get them started, and I'm not one to walk away from a good conversation. We might even talk about the weather while we're at it. . . ."

Chig thought she heard Uncle Elwin whistling as he loped off to his truck. There was no mistaking Willy's broad smile when he left to do his chores at home. Chig settled in to clean cans and was soon lost in thought. So much had happened in a few short days.

"Miss Kalpin?" The voice was quiet, so quiet Chig might have ignored it, putting it down to her imagination, if she hadn't seen a slight, rangy fellow standing nearby.

"Sir?" she asked. Then she recognized him. The hobo from the 10:40. She hadn't seen him since the train wreck, but it appeared that Niplak agreed with him. He was wearing a well-pressed work shirt, much-mended but clean trousers, and a soft cap. The cap went quickly into one hand as he made an elegant bow. Such manners were scarce in Niplak, and Chig wasn't sure how to react. In her silence, Mr. Newt continued.

"I'm most appreciative of the way you saved my life."

"Me?" said Chig. "I didn't save you. Miss Barkus did."

"Well," said he, "as Miss Barkus is quick to point out, she would never have thrown a rope my way if you hadn't brought my presence to her attention in the first place."

Chig only nodded.

"I am mighty thankful," he went on, "that Miss Barkus took your 'Looky there!' seriously. If she hadn't, I fear I might be feeding the fishes in that creek of yours."

Mr. Newt glanced beyond Chig to the free store's shelves. "Good to see that you were able to salvage so many of my traveling companions. It's a pity the labels are missing," he said, winking, "but we who live by the rails must be ready for the unexpected."

With that he bowed again. "I'll be forever in your debt, Chig Kalpin, forever in your debt." Then he slipped into the shadows behind the sorghum mill and was gone.

It was high time, Chig thought, to be going home herself. She would welcome a long, slow walk along familiar byways to sort things out. But as she rounded the dry goods store, a shiny black Dodge pulled up alongside her.

"Excuse me," a man said, rolling down the window, "could you tell me where I might find a Miss Minerva Kalpin?"

It was almost too much for Chig to take. She half considered pointing down the road and saying, "The Kalpin place is thataway," just to give herself a moment's rest. But instead, she fessed up.

"You found her," she said. "That's me."

The man looked Chig up and down. "I didn't expect you to be quite so petite," he said, shutting off the engine. He said that word *petite* just as Mama did. Chig warmed to him at once.

"Well, sir," she said, "I wasn't expecting you at all."

"No? Perhaps my letter was lost in the flooding. Half the state is underwater—and under a state of emergency. That's why I'm here. I started out in emergency relief, you know."

Chig didn't know but thought it impolite to say so.

"Harry Hopkins," he said, extending a hand, "WPA."

Was WPA after a person's name like M.D.? No, Chig decided. The only possible explanation was this: Harry Hopkins must be from the Works Progress Administration. But how had he known to come to Niplak? And how had he known her name? Had Mrs. FDR told him about her? It just could be.

"I've only got a minute," Hopkins said. "The president sent me out to view the flood damage, and Mrs. Roosevelt asked me to look you up, too. The state WPA man should be out here in a week or two, choosing a site and hiring workers. You'll have a new post office, I estimate, in little more than a year."

Chig managed a not too trembly handshake and a quiet but audible "Thank you" before Mr. Hopkins slid back behind the wheel and revved up the engine. "Fine little town you have here," he said.

Chig looked around and smiled. "Yep," she said, "it sure is."

19

SANDWICHES, SHOES, AND SPURTS

Was that fella for real? Chig wondered. She had no reason to disbelieve except for the colossal unlikeliness of it all. That a bigwig from the WPA should turn up in Niplak, looking for her. Even if he and all he had said did turn out to be for real, Chig was still a Kalpin, just like her great-great-granddaddy. Kalpins were humble about their accomplishments. Chig wasn't going to toot her own horn. Plus, what had happened was just unlikely enough that she feared jinxing it if she spoke of it.

So she didn't. She didn't mention it that night at dinner. She didn't say a word when Uncle Elwin heard from postal headquarters that Niplak was in line to get its very own P.O. Nor did she bring it up when the state WPA man motored into town a week later.

Chig went to Niplak soon after he arrived. A crowd gathered around him when he looked at building sites and took down names of men to hire for the work crew. At last Chig found a quiet moment by the big rock to introduce herself.

"I'm Miss Minerva Kalpin," she said, holding out her hand.

"Howdy-do," he answered, giving her a firm, friendly shake. But it was clear he didn't recognize her name.

Chig never even mentioned it to Miss Barkus. She never spoke of Harry Hopkins and his special errand to find Miss Minerva Kalpin, letter writer. Not even when she might have slipped it casually into the conversation.

"Seems a miracle that Niplak should get its own P.O. right after you asked for one, doesn't it?" Chig's teacher said one day after the last bell.

"Yep," Chig agreed.

"Pity we haven't heard from Mrs. Roosevelt."

"Yep," Chig said.

"I'm relieved you don't sound too disappointed," Miss Barkus said. "I expect Mrs. FDR gets piles of letters and can't be expected to answer them all."

"Well," said Chig, "what's one letter when we're getting the whole P.O.?"

"That's a fine way to look at it, Chig," Miss Barkus

said, and the two sat for a moment in silence. Chig could have mentioned Mr. Hopkins then, but she didn't. And not talking didn't feel bad as it had once, when she'd known all about the vernal equinox and her mouth had clamped shut. No, it was as if she were a magician, steeped in the secrets of the ancients, but choosing to reveal only so much at a time. Instead of making her feel small, this time not saying a word made her feel big.

After school and on Saturdays when she found the time, Chig filled a basket with cans from the free store. She set off for some of the more distant cabins, ones that Uncle Elwin's rural route didn't reach. "That you, Chig?" Editha Evans shouted one sunny Saturday.

"Yep."

Chig meant to leave the cans on the porch next to Editha's rocker and hightail it home, but Editha invited her to set a spell. "Take a load off," she said, pointing to a rough bench.

"Don't mind if I do." Chig shot a few sideways glances at Editha's cane, but it looked to be taking a rest too.

"Thanks to you, I got me a new boarder," Editha said.

"Thanks to me?" Chig gazed at a dusty red hen pecking in the dirt beyond the porch.

"I mean Newt," said Editha.

"Newt?"

"Sure," Editha explained, sucking contentedly on her pipe. "That Mr. Newt of yours is at the Saw and Haul right now choosing boards for my new henhouse. Turns out he's quite a handy fellow for being as genteel as he is."

"That so?" Chig asked.

"Yep," said Editha. "He's offered to help me with chores round the house in return for a perch to sleep on and a place at the table."

Chig suddenly wished she'd brought more canned goods.

"Says he was a broker in wheat futures up in Chicago," Editha went on, "but there ain't been no future in wheat for a long time. So he got handy."

"Always a future in that," said Chig, "leastways around Niplak."

"So it seems, my girl. So it seems."

The view from Editha's porch was pure loveliness. Redbud and dogwood sprinkled purples and whites all through the woods. Green buds were forming on the ends of tree branches. Finally, the world was drying out. Chig took it all in and gave Editha a bit of company. Neither said a word, but their silence was comfortable. It was broken only by the chug of a truck struggling up what passed for a road.

"Whoa, Nelly!" Editha cried as the truck finally

lurched to stop near her ruined henhouse. Mr. Newt and Ed Beemis hopped out of the cab and began unloading newly sawn planks.

"Go make sure they do a neat job of it, Chig," Editha said, whapping her cane in the air.

So Chig reluctantly walked toward the men and the growing pile of boards. She welcomed the chance to talk with Mr. Newt, but she hadn't seen Ed Beemis since the Great Niplak Train Disaster, not even at church on Sundays.

"Hey," she said, still keeping her distance.

Mr. Newt smiled and waved. Ed paused to wipe a bead of sweat from his forehead with a red bandana.

"See you got at least one of your hankies back," she said.

"Got 'em all back," he said, "just like you promised." He sounded calm, if a little breathless from the work. Maybe he didn't hold it against her that she'd ordered him around that day at Gibson's. But come to think of it, she hadn't seen him at Gibson's since then.

"You been keeping yourself kinda scarce, Ed," said Chig.

"Lots of work these days at the Saw and Haul, even with my dad on the mend. And then there's my flock to look after."

"Your flock?" Chig asked.

"Yep," Ed answered. "I'm helping the Reverend Whittle start a church in Needmore. Seems there's lots of souls to be saved down that way."

"That so?" Chig asked. If there were parts of Ed's own soul that could use saving, Chig didn't mention them. She didn't speak of his marble-playing soul or his pig-squealing soul. Or of any of the dark parts of his soul that had all too recently found pleasure in tormenting her. And once again, keeping quiet made her feel good, not invisible.

Soon Chig had to hurry on home. Her daddy needed her there. It was going to be a busy season. Mr. Kalpin was looking forward to spring planting. And he'd just been called up by the road crew. After that he'd be working with the WPA to build Niplak's first post office. Willy's father and the Settle twins had hired on for the job too. So had the fathers or older brothers of quite a few scholars at the Niplak school.

Until ground was broken for the new P.O., many fathers and brothers worked hard to rebuild the railroad bridge. Buzz Hawthorne and Ed Beemis at the Saw and Haul supplied new timbers. And after a disastrous meeting with a muddy stretch of road, Mr. Thorough hired Uncle Elwin to chauffeur him from his hotel in Martinsville to the bridge and back each day. It was short-term work, but good-paying. It added mightily to the reserves around Niplak.

Even Ogden Newt eventually hired on with the bridge crew, although from what Chig heard from the Settle twins, he was still a bit skittish around water. Maybe he'd be happier once he started work at the P.O., on firm ground. Chig could scarcely imagine how a man could give up the mystery of life on the rails, but if a person were to give it up for something, a life in Niplak wouldn't be half bad. She meant to ask him about his adventures as a hobo one Saturday after she'd dropped off the last of her load of cans and checked the dwindling remaining stock at the free store. As she walked home from town, she spied Mr. Newt taking the path to the Niplak school.

She followed him, hoping to catch both him and Miss Barkus for a chat. Chig's teacher was often at the schoolhouse of a Saturday, coaching her spelling-bee team or correcting algebra and geometry lessons. Soon Chig nudged the door open and peered in.

Miss Barkus was indeed there, seated at her desk. Ogden Newt was leaning over her, a small jar of flowers held in one hand.

After the Great Niplak Train Disaster, Mr. Newt had politely thanked Chig, the Settle twins, Buzz Hawthorne, and just about every other soul in Niplak for saving him. But as far as Chig could tell from the schoolhouse door, Mr. Newt seemed bent on spending the rest of his life thanking Miss Barkus.

"I believe the dogtooth violet is a member of the lily family," Newt said, his hand shaking slightly.

Chig was too far away to be seen, or to see the delicate

yellow flowers rising above their mottled green leaves. But she could make out Miss Barkus's shy, sweet smile. Chig's face burned red—as if she'd gotten a fresh chigger bite, but with none of the sting and none of the itch.

Mail deliveries were hefty once the creek was re-bridged and the 10:40 began running again. Everyone seemed to be getting mail, even Chig. The paper she found one day in the family's mailbox held as much mystery as any of the messages Chandu the Magician received while consulting his crystal ball. "Package for Chig," it said. "Too big for the mailbox. Being held at Gibson's." Hubie read over her shoulder and insisted on tagging along. This time he managed to avoid upsetting all the pails and eagerly grabbed the package from Mr. Gibson's hands. Chig let him carry it outside to the big rock, where Willy was dozing. The sun was shining warmly on the rock's smooth face, and the walk home was too long for Chig to wait. She had to open the package right away.

Willy awakened and handed over his pocketknife without being asked. Chig sawed at the string. She dug at the wrapping until a slip of paper fell out. Chig recognized at once her aunt Dorothea's handwriting:

Girlie,

Heard you made Niplak proud. Can't wait to come down for a visit and see if you've had a spurt. (Been eating your growing foods, haven't you?) Found the enclosed in the clearance basement at L. S. Ayres. Don't you dare tell me you've grown so much they don't fit!

Love and hugs,
Aunt Dorothea

The shoes were made of soft brown leather. They laced up to midankle. They had what were known as fashion heels—not so high as to cause a scandal at the Church of Our Redeemer on Sunday, but high enough to make a girl like Chig feel almost tall.

She tried them on. She turned around. She pushed up high on tiptoe, and then she blinked. For the first time in her life, Chig could see over the top of the big rock. It was a whole different view of the world, but not so different, she figured, that she couldn't get used to it.

She stuffed the shoes back into the wrapping for the walk home. Niplak's mud crop was bountiful enough that she didn't want to chance losing them.

"Put them on," Mama insisted when Chig unwrapped the package again.

"Oh, my!" she said when she saw them on Chig's feet.

"Why, they make you look like a little lady," said Daddy.

Chig wore her new shoes until Mama pulled a pencil end out of the junk drawer and Daddy had the children line up by the closet door. How long had it been since Chig had checked her height? She couldn't remember. When had she gotten so busy that she'd forgotten to check for a spurt?

Em went first, then Hubie. They were predictably tall. Finally Chig pressed her bare heels back and set her shoulders straight against the door. She looked ahead calmly.

"Will you look at that," Daddy said.

"My lands," said Mama.

"What is it?" asked Chig.

"See for yourself," said Daddy, gently turning Chig around. There it was. The new pencil mark was drawn a full inch higher than the last one.

"Probably just my hair," Chig said.

"Can't be all hair," said Mama, looking Chig up and down.

"Nope," said Daddy. "The pencil doesn't lie. That's a spurt if I ever saw one."

As the school year neared its end, scholars were still spending lunchtimes comparing notes on the label-less mystery cans.

"We had canned salmon and lima beans for supper last night," said Alberta.

"We put chopped peaches in our pancakes," said Chig. "Em ate five of them!"

"Mmmm," Alberta said. When something sounded that good, there really wasn't much more you could say about it.

Even Pearl Huddleston had tasted some of the mystery food. "We had a can of tuna yesterday," Willy said, "and I let her have a spoonful. Should've seen her wolf it down!"

The Hilltopper's cargo also appeared in lunch bags. Pineapple-slice and peanut butter sandwiches were popular. Green beans with tartar sauce, and baked beans with slices of Bermuda onion (heavy on the salt and pepper) were deemed acceptable. Nearly every student could tell of the excitement of opening a can of deviled ham—a spread that stood confidently on its own. Chig and Willy still traded halves. That way, each could savor just a little bit more of what the world had to offer.

At recess on the last day of class, Chig held back from the crowd of scholars spilling out into the schoolyard. She wanted to tell Miss Barkus about her spurt and about Ed's flock of souls to be saved. But she never got a chance. Instead, Miss Barkus thrust a small oblong box into Chig's lap as the two sat by the stove.

"Go ahead," said Miss Barkus. "Open it."

Chig did and found inside a set of five brand-new pencils, not even sharpened yet. And each one was engraved in gold with the letters CMK.

"Oh, Miss Barkus!" said Chig. "I can't take these. I'm not like FDR!"

"You're close enough for me, Chig Kalpin. Now, go along. Scoot! Get out there and kick up some dirt with the other scholars."

Chig did just that, first putting the box of pencils carefully in her desk. The sun on the schoolyard was hot and bright after a morning of light fog. Chig and Willy played a quick game of ringer, but only for fairsies, not for keepsies. There would be plenty of warm days come summer for trading marbles back and forth.

"Scholars," Miss Barkus said after her bell had called them in. "Normally I wait until the start of a new school term to make seat assignments. But two of our scholars have made such progress and shown such growth that I will make an exception."

Miss Barkus strode to the middle row, the heels of her shoes clicking jauntily on the wooden floor and her pointer tapping lightly on the desktops. Her pointer stopped at two vacant desks. Most recently, they'd been home to Jimbo and Theo Limp. But the twins and the rest of the Limp family had moved down to Kentucky to care for a sick grandma. "Chig. Willy. You may move to your new seats."

Chig sat tall. Even Willy looked more than half interested. Miss Barkus was talking, but Chig barely heard a word. It was her teacher's usual year-end speech, and Chig had heard enough of them that she could probably be excused from listening closely just this once. So much to look at! The backs of other scholars' heads! A new desktop with new carvings to examine! It was quite a change, after all those years, to be smack dab in the middle of the action. But it was the kind of change you could get used to pretty fast if you put your mind to it.

Chig tried at last to put her mind to listening.

"Scholars," Miss Barkus said, "you are dismissed!"

"*Yee-haw!*"

For as long as Chig had been going to the Niplak school, Willy Huddleston had greeted the last day of class this way. He hollered as if he meant to take the roof right off the building. And for once, Chig Kalpin joined in.

AUTHOR'S NOTE

WHERE do stories come from? The setting for the story of Chig is the southern Indiana of my childhood, a place of gravel roads, much mud, dogwood trees blooming in springtime, and hillsides painted with the colors of leaves in fall. But the events and characters in that setting have many sources—tales half remembered, a scrap of newspaper, recipes for strange sandwiches, letters from children struggling through hard times, and the sound of a gong.

The greatest single source for *Chig and the Second Spread* is my father, Henry Swain. Hank grew up during the Great Depression, and from the way he describes it—as a time of visiting neighborly and feasting on homemade cottage cheese or apple dumplings—I always thought it was the *great* depression. While I was growing up, he entertained me and my sisters with tales of a lady who checked to see how well he painted behind her bathtub, of Sunday dinners with family, and—on a more somber note—of folks so poor they had only one thing to spread between the covers of their sandwiches.

The character of Minerva "Chig" Kalpin came from an obituary I read in my hometown newspaper. Genevra Irene "Chig" Owens (1917–2000) was, according to the obituary, "so tiny her grandfather compared her to a 'red chigger.'" Thus was born her nickname, Chig. When she first started walking to the one-room Owl Creek school, she was "still small," the obituary reported, "and would become bogged down in the mud." Like the fictional Chig Kalpin, Chig Owens's mother came to "get her out of the muck."

Other events in *Chig and the Second Spread* have their own sources. In a cookbook called *Dining During the Depression*, edited by Karen Thibodeau, I read of how a train derailment during a flood gave one community the gift of unlabeled "mystery meals" in a can. The taste that my mother, Mardi Coman Swain, had for unlikely combinations such as tartar sauce and leftover green beans between slices of bread inspired many of the strange sandwiches that found their way into lunch pails at the Niplak school.

Chig's decision to write to First Lady Eleanor Roosevelt was inspired in part by *Dear Mrs. Roosevelt: Letters from Children of the Great Depression*, edited by Robert Cohen. The letters in this collection, often full of worry, provided a counterpoint to my father's mainly happy memories of the depression. Mrs. Roosevelt did not have the resources to respond to all the requests for help from children. Unlike

Chig, most letter writers received only a form reply from one of the First Lady's staff members.

Perhaps those children, like Chig, wished for magical powers to solve their problems. Radio heroes such as Chandu the Magician captured the imagination of children during the Great Depression. My parents still tell of the shiver of anticipation and fear they felt when the gong sounded at the beginning of each episode. Chandu learned the secrets of the ancients, but Chig learned something simpler and perhaps more precious—the power of believing in herself and in her ability to be the big person she wanted to be.

Gwenyth Swain grew up hearing her father's colorful stories about his childhood during the Great Depression. After he told her of a family so poor they had only one spread on their sandwiches, Gwenyth knew she wanted to write a story of her own. The character of Chig was inspired by a woman from her Indiana hometown who as a girl was so small, folks said she was no bigger than a red chigger. The author of a number of nonfiction books for young readers, Gwenyth Swain lives with her husband and their two young children in St. Paul. This is her first novel.